Old Rosa

Old Rosa

A NOVEL
IN TWO STORIES

Reinaldo Arenas

TRANSLATED FROM THE SPANISH BY

Ann Tashi Slater

AND

Andrew Hurley

GROVE PRESS

NEW YORK

Grove Press
841 Broadway
New York, New York 10003

Library of Congress Cataloging-in-Publication Data
Arenas, Reinaldo, 1943–
[Vieja Rosa. English]
Old Rosa; and, The brightest star: two novels/by Reinaldo
Arenas; translated from the Spanish by Ann Tashi Slater and Andrew
Hurley. —1st ed.
Translation of: La vieja Rosa, and of: Arturo, la estrella más
brillante.
I. Arenas, Reinaldo, 1943–   Arturo, la estrella más brillante.
English. 1989.   II. Title.   III. Title: Old Rosa.   IV. Title:
Brightest star.
PQ7390.A72A6   1989
863—dc19   88-21421
ISBN 0-8021-3406-8 (pbk.)

Designed by Irving Perkins Associates

Manufactured in the United States of America

First Edition 1989
First Paperback Edition 1994

10 9 8 7 6 5 4 3 2 1

Contents

Old Rosa

TRANSLATED FROM THE SPANISH

BY

Ann Tashi Slater

IN THE END SHE WENT OUT TO THE YARD, ALMOST enveloped in flames, leaned against the tamarind tree that no longer flowered, and began to cry in such a way that the tears seemed never to have begun, but to have been there always, flooding her eyes, producing that creaking noise, like the noise of the house at the moment when the flames made the strongest posts totter and the flashing frame came down in an enormous crackling that pierced the night like a volley of fireworks. She went on crying, and her face, shrouded in a reddish halo, looked at times like the face of a little girl lost in the middle of one of those storms that only occur in hallucinatory illustrations accompanying stories of witches and other phantasmagorias, which she had never read. But now and then, when the flames exploded almost before her eyes, singeing her lashes, her face lit up with all the features that time had undertaken to etch there. Then it could be seen, clearly, that this was an old woman. And had one of the neighbors passed by, he would have confirmed that this woman could be none other than Old Rosa. The brands, still flaming, were leaping into the air and tumbling down over the towering weeds in the yard. The fire was feeding upon itself, rising up all around in a sudden surge and threatening to strike the woman, making her breathing more difficult every moment. She was surrounded by the flames, and had she screamed, it is possible that no one would have heard her cry, indistinguishable in the snapping of the weeds and the explosion of the trees, which were even then dissolving in the air, transformed into evanescent swirls of ash. She was surrounded by fire, and in other times, terrified, she might have said, or at least might have imagined: *My God, this is hell.* And even if she had felt lost she might have started to pray. But now she was not praying, not calling out, not even seeing the fire that was already leaping impatiently up to her skirt. She was seeing, and this is true, other realities even more important to her. At her side there were not flames, not weeds, not crackling, not even the smoldering ruins of the house; and she was only Rosa, for it would not have occurred to anyone to attach to this remarkably young woman (with those terrific legs she had mysteriously preserved without a scratch) the epithet *old.* She was only Rosa. Rosa, Tano's daughter; Rosa, the little one in the family; Rosa, the one who had actually listened to transistor radios; Rosa, the one with the perfect legs. Rosa, Pablo's woman. And Pablo arrived, as he did every Sunday, and headed toward the house, jingling his spurs, whistling, ambling with his young colt's gait that was far more graceful than the gait of the horse he rode away on every afternoon, after having chatted for a moment with the old man, after having grasped her hands in his and asked her to let him sit on the sofa, next to her, for the wedding would be very soon. But she, as always, not only forbade him to sit at her side, she also withdrew her hand and recited the words *honor,* and *family,* and *respect.* And Pablo moved uneasily in his chair, and when it came time to leave he stood up very solemnly, with his hands in his pockets. And now, the explosion of the last uprights supporting the house merged with the explosion of the chicken coops and the custard apple tree, and a flock of screeching birds fell singed before her unseeing eyes. The tamarind tree glowed red, and the lowest branches crackled softly at the touch of the first flames. It was the day of the wedding, and she went, as always, to give the hens their corn, and she felt for those who were ready to lay, and with a stone she killed a rat that was eating the newborn chicks; then she went to the well, drew a bucket of cold water, and washed herself in the bathhouse, behind the shed for the calabashes and the corn. The guests were arriving, and she greeted them all, and offered them coconut nougats and a punch that was quite watery, almost a lemonade. And the house was filling up with people, until even the Pupo sisters were there. *Those miserable whores,* she thought. And she became furious. And she ordered her mother to throw them out of the house or there would be no wedding. But just then Pablo arrived from the mango grove; he had tied the horse up and was already in the breezeway. The bridegroom entered, and pandemonium broke out among the guests; the youngest ones ran to greet him, and patted him on the back, and spoke to him, smiling, whispering in his ears. How lucky you are, one of the Pupo girls dared to say to her, maliciously, looking toward Pablo. But she did not answer; she averted her eyes, turned her back, and went to the kitchen, where her mother and other old women from the countryside were preparing the meal and the sweets. There aren't going to be enough coconut nougats, she said. Shortly afterward an automobile could be seen coming down over the plain. All the boys went out onto the porch. Here comes the priest, they shouted. And they ran up to the fence, and solemnly watched how that prominent man, dressed in a black frock and sandals, got out of the car, greeted them, and started to walk toward the house. The priest entered the living room, and everyone stood up; some of the men crossed themselves, and the women carried their little ones to him so he could bless them. The priest ascertained how many children had not been baptized and proposed a collective baptism for the following week. Then the wedding began. Rosa saw

5

herself surrounded by the lights of tall candles glittering between the areca palms that her mother had arranged on the makeshift altar; she looked at Pablo, who was now watching very solemnly as the priest gave the benediction with a raised hand; beyond him she noted the bowed heads of the guests, the boys perched in the windows, the tearful old women blowing their noses in the corners, the Pupo girls, sad, watching her from the middle of the room, where the afternoon glow spilled in through the doorway and flooded over them, giving them a look of complete desolation. Then she stared at them fixedly, as if challenging them, and smiled to herself. At midnight the two of them, she and Pablo, left the house; he in front, on the horse's saddle; she on the rump, holding fast to the man's waist. The horse bucked, Pablo spurred it; and the three of them disappeared over the plain. Later they picked up the main road. When they came to a grove of trees beside a brook, Pablo reined in the horse, jumped down, took her by the waist, and seated her in the tall grass. I can't hold out till we get to the house, he said. We're going to stop here, and afterward we'll go on. Rosa, we're married now, he continued. And he was breathing heavily. And his voice came out very hoarse and low. She, still dazed by the wild horseback ride, did not know what to say. There's still a very long way to go, he said, and he pulled her to him. And she felt something like another powerful arm rubbing against her thighs. And suddenly she threw the man off, looked at him, almost terrified, slapped him across the face, and took off running toward the horse, which was impassively eating daisies by the brook. Very solemnly, they went on their way, and at dawn they arrived at the house. He started to prepare coffee, and she in the meantime took off her shoes, heard the crickets chirping, and thought happily that it would soon be morning. Then they entered the bedroom. A tongue of fire cut through the crown-of-thorns plants, carbonized the dead horse slumped across the bed of yellow irises, and broke like an incandescent wave over the guinea grass, which exploded into flame

6

amidst the cackling hens fluttering madly in fright; the flames kept spreading, they cut through the wire fence and reached the old patch of wild pineapples, which instantly began to burn like a long wick drenched in gasoline. The fire reached the cultivated land, and the already yellowing cornfield trembled with fury, vanishing in a dark glow. A few owls, blinded, flew about in a frenzy, sometimes tumbling to the ground where the circle of flame was mightiest. Old Rosa went on crying in a measured flow, neither increasing nor decreasing the intensity, paying no attention to the fire that occasionally seemed to want to leap up to her hands. Nothing happened the first night. Pablo took off his shirt, lay down next to her, and ran his hands over her hips. She remained in her clothes, and when he went to take off his pants, she screamed. I'm tired, she said then, calmer; tomorrow will be different. He stopped unbuttoning his pants, sat down on the bed, grasped her hands, and pulling her to him, again lay down at her side. Rosa kept her eyes open and looked toward the rafters, which were lost in the darkness. And she wondered if it was not a sin in spite of everything, in spite of being married and in spite of the fact that the priest had blessed it. Holy Mother of God, she thought, maybe I just wasn't born for such things. With that she fell asleep. In the morning, Pablo woke her, bringing her a cup of coffee in bed. She stood up in her crumpled dress, took the coffee, and went out to the yard. Pablo went to her; very slowly he pressed against her from behind, slipping his hands over her breasts. You don't have a single saint in the bedroom, she said then, not looking at him. Tomorrow we're going to bring mine. As soon as night fell they retired. Rosa threw herself into bed, still in the dress she had worn all day, but Pablo, before she could protest, took off all his clothes and lay down naked at her side. For a long time the two of them were silent. Little by little she made out his face, his tousled hair falling over his eyes; then, hardly daring to breathe, she lowered her gaze and contemplated his hairy chest, his waist; and at last she brought herself to look

7

down at his thighs, and there she lingered, terrified before that prominent muscle that rose, radiant, between the man's legs. Pablo did not speak; he lay face up with his hands crossed under his head, staring at the ceiling with unseeing eyes; and although several times he felt the desire to rip off her dress, he remained motionless, his erect organ bearing witness to the almost painful need to penetrate her. Thus they passed the night. But at dawn, he could stand it no longer, and almost crying, he pressed his face to Rosa's and started biting her with such fury that she was suddenly disconcerted. Animal, she said immediately. But he, infuriated, groped for the woman's body with his mouth, clutched her hips; finally he reached her knees and kissed her thighs and her feet. Animal, she kept repeating as she felt him panting over her body. And although she had to make a great effort not to cry out, she endured in silence. Afterward she resumed her chant, *Animal, animal,* but this time the words sounded far away and had a tone of resignation. The next day they did not get up; when it was growing dark, Pablo, in the spasms of a pleasure repeated beyond counting, heard the woman saying to him: *Tomorrow we're definitely going to get the saints.* They went. When they returned from the trip, the basket packed with plaster figures, portraits of virgins, silver crosses and hundreds of chains, medallions and busts of virtually unknown martyrs and saints, Rosa began to set up a great altar in a corner of the bedroom. She spent the whole day arranging the figures, putting up long shelves to hold the largest images, nailing vases full of flowers to the beams; and when at last, in the afternoon, dripping with sweat, she completed the monumental installation, she threw herself on her knees and prayed for two hours. She asked, before all else, that the livestock multiply, that prosperity never abandon them; then she prayed for Pablo, that he stay strong. Oh, God, and don't let him grow old. Or me, God. And then her entreaty was not an entreaty but a kind of anguished protest. It was growing dark and still she had not completed her prayer. It

8

was then that she sensed, or almost imagined, the presence of a watchful shadow at her back. She quickly looked behind her. But there was no one. She was alone in the room. Sunlight filtered through the window to the bed, bathing it in a pale glow that was rapidly dissolving in the shadows. And suddenly she felt an unfamiliar fear. And she left the room almost at a run. Pablo, she said from the living room. Pablo, she said again and again, and went out to the yard. There he was, carefully closing the gate that led to the pasture. What's the matter, he said to her, and pulled her to him. Nothing, she said. And the two of them went into the house. It was completely dark, and Pablo lit the oil lamp. . . . Their first child was strong and healthy, and they named him Pablo Armando (although they always called him just Armando). Another man to work, said Rosa, and Pablo smiled. Then came Rosa Maria (she was known as Rosa), blond, almost albino, but very healthy. And four years later Arturo arrived, a seven-month baby given to crying, with constant fevers; it was a miracle that he survived. Thy will be done, said Rosa as she stood before the promontory of the saints at the end of the forty days of confinement. The following year they had another son who did not cry when he was born. The midwife said he was blind. He died the day after his birth. Rosa, prostrate on the bed, could barely speak; her body was racked by convulsions; and for a moment she thought that she too was going to die. If I survive this, she said— and now she was not addressing God or anyone in particular—I will never have another baby. She survived. And so that she would not get pregnant, she never again had relations with Pablo. In vain did the man heave at midnight, pace naked about the room with his erect organ pointing in all directions. For more than a month he performed the same rites. He undressed, lay down next to her, and remained in a state of arousal for hours, touching his member, sobbing, begging Rosa to satisfy him. At first he held to the hope that things would work themselves out as they had the first time, after the wedding; but Rosa held firm and paid no attention to the demands of the man, who at times beat the pillow or stamped the floor in rage, and she even began to get used to these outbursts, and ended up falling asleep, lulled by the sound of the heaving and groaning, summoning, before closing her eyes, the image of that swollen phallus pulsing in the darkness. As soon as she fell asleep, Pablo started to masturbate at her side; then he too drifted off to sleep. Pig, she said to him once when she was awakened by the creaking of the bed and saw him relieve himself, gasping, Pig, she said again, and went back to sleep. From that point on, he did not masturbate. And later on, in bed, the two of them would speak of the weather, of the crops, of the children, who were growing and needed shoes. Then they would go to sleep. The farm was producing more all the time. The two of them got up early and went out to the fields; they plowed the earth, herded the cattle from one pasture to another, built new fences. After a time, Rosa decided that it would be a good idea to hire some day laborers. She herself chose among the poorest and hardest-working peasants, those whom she could pay less and who produced more. She herself, as soon as she had hired them, inspected their work; she cooked for them, subtracting the cost of lunch from the day's wages; and she kept the accounts of all the workers in a yellowed datebook her mother had given her on the day of the wedding. Little by little Pablo was losing his position as husband and man of the house. He had already given up having relations with Rosa, and now he wandered about the farm or fell asleep in the canefields; sometimes he went as far as the river and remained for hours watching the current. He had gone there with Rosa when they were first married. They had undressed and taken a leisurely dip in the river. Then the two of them climbed out onto the bank, and without saying a word, lay down in the grass, not feeling the mites, hearing, if anything, their own accelerated breathing; neither was it necessary to speak when he moved onto her, slowly, first placing one leg over her leg, then resting his hands on her hips, finally penetrating, smoothly, now without difficulty, that familiar body. And although they did not fall asleep, they lay there for a while floating in a hazy lethargy, amid a procession of trees, the river, the grass tickling their bodies. But now he was alone, and he was not watching the waters that swept past before his eyes; and the countryside, being the same, was different; and the stirring of the least blade of grass, or the commotion of a bird, was like an obbligato flowing beneath his sadness. . . . One day, Pablo went to town as usual, to sell the crops, but he did not return until dawn. Swinging wildly, he broke down the door and entered the house, knocking over furniture and laughing raucously. He was completely drunk. Rosa, with the three children around her, watched him for a second. Then she started to insult him. A whole string of offenses (that had nothing to do with his behavior) reached Pablo's ears, but he was not even listening. Afterward, Rosa took him roughly by the shoulders and led him to the bed. She undressed him, covered him with a blanket, and stood there watching him; she blew out the candle and lay down at his side. The children had already fallen asleep; the alarm clock on the cabinet was ticking almost in time with the croaking of the frogs in the lake. Occasionally the odor of fresh earth drifted in through the cracks in the walls. The radiance of the night lay over the husband's face, disclosing the countenance of a defenseless adolescent. Rosa sat up in bed, the sheets slipped over her breasts and left her naked to the waist. Hardly daring to breathe, she drew back the blanket that enveloped Pablo; his body, milky in the luminescence of the night, seemed to glow before her eyes. Suddenly she saw her uplifted hand poised to caress, almost tenderly, the man's thighs. As her hand slowly slipped down, she thought that the commotion of the frogs had ceased, and she remained still, her hand motionless on the man's body. But then the commotion of all the animals of the dawn seemed to surge forth more violently. The odor of drenched earth grew stronger; she inhaled deeply, and her hand moved smoothly but firmly toward the part of the man that she had tried so often to imagine as a little girl. She was in ecstasy, her hand touching that wondrous region; and if for a moment the pandemonium of the night had died down, it might have been possible to hear the mounting agitation of her blood. Then she looked toward the corner of the room where all the saints rose up, and she saw them emerge like hallucinatory figures in the midst of the darkness; and for a moment she saw a kind of glow trembling among those unmoving bodies. She immediately withdrew her hand; frightened, she pulled the sheets over her head and started to pray frantically. The next day, Rosa put a bed in the furthest room of the house, next to the corn shed. It'll be better if you sleep here, she said to her husband. He did not reply. He walked to that cramped room, where the rats scurried back and forth constantly, and threw himself on the cot, which let out three short groans. Rosa went to the altar, followed by the three children. There she made them kneel down. And the four of them intoned the *Ave Maria*. . . . Things continued to thrive at the farm. The corn crop was abundant; prices had risen; and the Christmas Eve celebration was extraordinary. Rosa had invited the whole family and some people who lived nearby. Seated at one end of the table, she was carving the suckling pig with remarkable precision, talking about the difficulty of getting calabash seeds for the spring crop. At midnight, when the laughter of the guests was at its noisiest, her mother called her to the yard and led her to the trees that grew near the well. Look, she said, gesturing toward the topmost boughs. Pablo was hanging from one of the highest branches of the custard apple tree. Rosa crossed herself. As she was saying, My God, she was thinking: *He did it to spoil my Christmas Eve. That's why he did it.* She had organized this celebration (in spite of the fact that the waste of money and food vexed her soul) to show the neighbors and her family her position. And also, she said, because this is the one celebration of the year you can't miss. Such were her thoughts. And now she watched her husband's body swaying imperceptibly under the bough of the tree. She took him down. Assumed the appropriate attitude. And entered the dining room, screaming. After her husband's death, Rosa seemed to worry even more about the farm. She spent most of the day in the fields, quarreling with the workers when they did not do things in the way she thought most efficient, railing against the weather when it interrupted the sowing of the corn with its unexpected downpours, throwing rocks at the cows that jumped the garden fence and ate the sweet potato shoots. As twilight fell she walked to the house, scolded the children if they had not done what she had ordered them to do; and finally she went to her room and threw herself on her knees in front of the altar. But now there was something in her manner of praying that was completely different; her words did not well up in a long supplication, invested with an unmistakable note of submission; her intonation did not seem that of a prayer but of an order. There was too much assurance in her voice. And sometimes, as she addressed the images that now had multiplied, anyone who happened to hear her from the living room might well have thought she was addressing one of her laborers in the field. Her children grew up listening to this authoritarian voice that spurred the men of the farm to action, that could order the hut under the ceiba tree torn down and made into charcoal. And so the children continued to grow; and if it was true that they had not come out as she might have wished, they obeyed her in everything, and this was a consolation. Armando was already eighteen; he went to town every afternoon and returned at dawn, sometimes in very high spirits, carried by the horse that knew the way and bore the boy's unconscious body. Rosa, the daughter, still dressed like a little girl and wore big blue ribbons in her hair, although she was fifteen; she spent most of her time, on her mother's orders, learning to embroider, and playing apathetically with the big, clumsy coconut dolls that certain Kings, who she knew very well did not exist, left by her pillow every year. And Arturo, the mysterious Arturo, spent the day in the tree branches, slumbering among the leaves, dreaming dreams that not even he could decipher; sometimes, at night, he sat down in a corner of the breezeway and stayed there for hours, whistling, his figure barely discernible in the penumbra. He was eleven years old, and he was the child Rosa worried about the most. But there's no reason to be alarmed, she said, trying to convince herself. She paid more attention to him than to the others; every month she took him to the doctor, and she made him sleep next to her, in the bedroom dominated by the figures of the saints. Sometimes, at dawn, she felt the boy tossing and turning in the sheets, and she would pull him to her; he would drift off to sleep, tightly swaddled against his mother's body. Then, in the approaching light, Rosa would hear the roosters crow, watch the darkness lifting, and there in bed, reflecting that she was in her house and that her children were sleeping near her, she would feel a great peace, a stillness indistinguishable from the silence of the dawn, emanating from the security of the stones of the house, from the freshness of the hour and the rhythmic breathing of her children. One night she discovered, in the midst of this great calm which she found inexplicable, that she was no longer young and that the people in those parts did not call her Rosa, but *Old Rosa*. They all considered Old Rosa one of the strangest and wealthiest women around. Some of the men felt proud to say that they worked for her. The enormous farm that she had expanded little by little, buying land from her neighbors, assuming mortgages, was now known simply as *Old Rosa's Place*. The number of workers continued to grow, the harvest yielded more every year. Later on, Old Rosa leased all the properties adjacent to her farm and rented them to sharecroppers. Her children continued to obey her in everything and tried not to upset her. Armando still went to town every night, and rumor had it that he was the boyfriend of almost all the girls in the neighborhood. Some neighbors said he was not just a boyfriend and that they had seen him leaving one of the nearby houses at midnight. When Old Rosa learned of this gossip, she smiled, saying: *That's why he's a man. I bet he doesn't have to force any woman to spread her legs for him.* . . . The daughter, after much pleading, convinced the mother to send her to study in town, and she went to stay with some distant relatives whom Old Rosa now supplied with meat, vegetables, and money. Arturo was growing skinnier and taller all the time; he was already the same height as his mother. When the two of them went to inspect the farm in the afternoon, it was very difficult to tell them apart from afar. Of her three children she loved Arturo the most. It was he who received the most expensive and useless presents; the boy's slightest whim became law; and in the house, when he was sleeping, everyone had to walk very softly and not scrape their chairs. Nevertheless, sometimes Old Rosa watched him distrustfully, and it seemed to her that her son was a stranger. And so, when Arturo insisted on buying a transistor radio that cost a bundle, and when he built a tower on one side of the house, ensconced himself there with the radio, and began to hang around with the local boys, Old Rosa's face became a little more grim. One day, while walking about the immense kitchen, she was surprised to discover that she was talking to herself and gesturing into the emptiness. She went out to the yard and saw the figure of her eldest son, *as handsome as a young colt,* disappearing on horseback around a bend in the road; and for a moment she did not see the son, but the father, and she raised a hand to her lips. Immediately she went to the bedroom, knelt brusquely at the altar, and began to pray. When she stood up it was already dark. The next day three strange men arrived at the house. Old Rosa observed them from the yard as they opened the gate, and she raised her hands to shield her eyes from the sun and get a better view of the visitors: they were three very young boys; they sported incipient beards and were dressed in tattered, dirty green uniforms that were much too big for them. Good afternoon, the three of them said. (At that moment Armando came out of the house.) What do you want, Old Rosa replied. One of them began to speak. That afternoon Old Rosa learned that there was war, that the country was in revolution; and that these ragged soldiers who were coming to ask her for a cow to eat (and she knew this without their saying it) were starving to death, were imagining they could overthrow the government with shotguns that were held tógether by wire and would surely explode in their hands when fired. So you want a cow, said Old Rosa, with a surly and distrustful look; well, all the cows here are milk cows, you better go somewhere else. We want to buy it, said one of them, and he touched his pockets as if to indicate money. Old Rosa looked at them, astonished. You name the price, said the one who had just spoken. Take them to the pasture and show them the barren cows, Old Rosa ordered Armando. The four young men disappeared in the direction of the pasture. She stood there watching after them for a moment. Then she went to the breezeway, and there she stopped, observing a hummingbird that was fluttering nervously over the bed of yellow irises. At that moment Arturo came down from his room. The radio was going full blast. Who were those people, said the boy. No one, replied the mother; some cattle dealers. She raised her voice to an incredible pitch and screamed: Once and for all will you turn off that damn radio. The boy went up to his room, but he did not turn off the radio. A few minutes later the four men returned. Armando was leading a heifer by a rope tied to its horns. He hitched the animal to one of the posts of the farmhouse and called to his mother. Old Rosa looked at the heifer, which was raising reddish dust as it pawed the ground with a hoof, and said: One hundred pesos. One of the young men took out the money and gave it to her. Good, she said, if you want I can give you a receipt. They said it was not necessary, and left. Armando accompanied them as far as the main road. When he returned, his mother was still in the breezeway, talking to herself in front of a chinaberry tree that was bursting with flowers. So they want to get rid of the government, she said now to her son. And she seemed to be inspecting the branches of the chinaberry. The son remained silent; he went to a corner of the breezeway and sat down slowly against the wall; he picked a very delicate blade of grass and raised it to his lips. I think you charged them too much for the heifer, he said, it wasn't even worth fifty pesos. But Old Rosa did not hear him; she had discovered an anthill near the trunk of the tree, and she was thinking: The ants will finish off the flowers again; I'll have to sprinkle some ash, or buy some insecticide. Then she went to the bedroom, tucked the money in the cabinet, and stood there looking at the plaster images. At the very instant she crossed herself she thought she heard a noise in a corner of the bedroom. She turned. And for a moment she thought she saw a kind of gigantic shadow that trembled fleetingly on one side of the bed. But the noise ceased, the shadow vanished in the air, and already she was not sure if she had seen or heard anything. God help us, she said in a loud voice. She crossed herself again and started her prayer. The radio music drifted in as if from a distant region, commingled with the whistling of Armando, who was still sitting in the breezeway. Finally, she left the bedroom. Bathed in the glow of the afternoon, she crossed the dining room; and dazzled by this radiance that no longer warmed her, she stood there and listened to the crowing of the roosters and the shouts of the workers who were herding the animals back to the corral. And she thought, without knowing why, that these noises, so familiar, sounded sad, different, although they were the same ones she had always heard. Afterward she went to the kitchen and ordered the servants to set the table. The next morning, when she called Armando to go milk the cows, no one answered. She entered her son's room and found the bed rumpled and empty. Immediately she went to the kitchen and drank a cup of coffee. Later Arturo appeared, drowsy. It looks like Armando went off with the rebels, Old Rosa said to him. And she served him coffee. Instinctively she caressed his tousled hair. So he's with them, she said afterward, as if excusing herself from blame. He'll come back. And she added: *If he survives.* Arturo watched his mother, fascinated. But how do you know, he asked then. Because I'm not an idiot, she said. And the son lowered his eyes. Then came the most difficult months. All the roads were blockaded, the crops could not be taken to town, the vegetables rotted in the fields; and as if this were not enough, a small plane that was bombarding the woodland every day demolished three of Old Rosa's coal cellars and killed one of her cows in the middle of the pasture. But Old Rosa did not sit still. She started to do business with some cattle rustlers who passed themselves off as rebels and sold the meat in town; she traded vegetables with the neighbors, and when they did not have money to pay, she put them to work clearing land on the farm. One day two rebels arrived at her house asking for help. Old Rosa looked at them very calmly. Then she began to speak. I am possibly the one person in this area who has cooperated most with the Revolution, she said. I have a relative in the Sierra— that is, if he's not dead by now, and me with one less son. The rebels departed, taking their leave in low voices. Thus the Christmas holidays arrived, and as she did every year, Old Rosa sat down at the table and prepared to celebrate the birth of Christ. The daughter had returned a few months earlier, when they closed the school and the students went on strike; she came back very loquacious and expounded some tiresome economic theses that Old Rosa did not understand but suspected were not very good for the security of her household. Only Arturo re-mained loyal and stayed with her; and although he still shut himself in his tower with his friends and listened to music until dawn, he did not bother her at all, and was incapable of opposing her in anything aside from not turning down the radio. With the two children at the table, and some neighbors whom she invited every year, Old Rosa carved the suckling pig, served the meal, and gave the signal to start the prayer. At midnight almost all the guests left; only Arturo's friends stayed on, completely drunk, and sat around the table talking and applauding Rosa, who was standing on a stool improvising a speech. Old Rosa, who had also drunk quite a bit, was feeling dizzy. Escaping that confusing clamor, she went to her bedroom, lit the oil lamp, and sat down on the bed, resting her hands on her knees. She stayed like that for a while, until suddenly she felt a sort of fluttering at her back again, but this time she did not even bother to look behind her. Anyway, it's only the red wine, she said to herself, trying to believe that idea. Then she put out the oil lamp and lay down. The uproar of her children and their guests drifted in from the dining room. Now they were parodying a type of children's song, their voices rising up, sometimes very off-key, with startling high notes, and then falling to a far-off babble. For a while she lay thinking about Armando. Actually, since the afternoon when the rebels first arrived, she had suspected that something was going to happen; and when she saw her son going off with the other young men in the direction of the pasture, her premonitions were already clear, and she thought: *The change is going to start with Armando.* That was why, the next day, when she saw that he had vanished, she did not scream or sound the alarm in the country-side; she simply accepted, as one accepts an inevitable catastrophe, that Armando had gone with the rebels. And although she had no news of him, something told her that he was alive and that one of these days he would appear at her door completely re-pentant of his escapade. For if there was one thing she was sure of, it was that those people, with their shotguns held together by rusty wire, would never win the war. Yes, without a doubt her son would return, tired, skinny, and smelly. And she would go out to the porch to welcome him. And she would pull him to her. And although she would reproach him for nothing at that mo-ment, she would look at him, and with that he would understand what she was saying to him: I knew all along you were going to come back; these are the ideas of lunatics or people who are starving to death and have nothing left to lose but their lives.

That was how it would be. And listening to the children singing (now they were at the bottom of the scale, babbling), she drifted off to sleep. Armando arrived the next week, tired, skinny, and smelly. But he was beaming with satisfaction: the Revolution had triumphed. He came with a group of rebels, shouting and firing in the air with those decrepit shotguns. They entered the breezeway. Old Rosa and her two children went out to welcome them. The racket was tremendous. All the neighbors had fallen in behind the young men, and were hugging them, and lifting them on their shoulders, and asking them for details of the different battles. Armando entered the living room and invited his friends to sit down. He went to the kitchen and ordered a cow killed instantly. Old Rosa followed him at a distance, blinking, a little timorous and distrustful; she wondered if it could really be true that this man who was ordering a cow killed, without checking with her, as if he were the owner of the farm, was her son. And she doubted it when she looked at him, more solid now, with broader shoulders, with that almost casual assurance and that strength with which he hugged her, leaving her breathless. But such reasonings were too obscure for her, and she felt her head pounding. He was and he was not. He had returned and he had remained. And above all, he had won the war. But how was it possible. And for a moment she thought she was being tricked, although she could grasp neither the source of the deception nor its magnitude. Dazed, she went out to the yard. Some men were leading a cow by a rope. That one's pregnant, said Old Rosa. Go to the pasture and get a different one. And she was gratified to see that they obeyed her, that they released the cow and took off again toward the fields. She had shown who was in charge of the farm. Nevertheless, from that day on, things no longer possessed for Old Rosa the invisible equilibrium they had maintained until then. The children were at home; the workers continued to toil, and the crops were abundant, but something had changed. And she noted, with concern, that people were now excessively optimistic; and some workers even left the farm without explanation, and did not come back, as in the past, to ask her the favor of hiring them again. Months later, her daughter went to the town to continue her studies; Armando no longer lived at home but seemed very worried about the farm. He was always going to meetings, organizing the peasants in various political groups. Once he went to Havana. He stayed in the capital for six months taking a course in political action. Only Arturo remained at home, listening tirelessly to the radio, indifferent to the comings and goings that Rosa could not make heads or tails of. For two years Old Rosa continued to observe the constant turmoil in the area. In the end many laborers left the farm for good and went to work at the local cooperative. So she took up the plow again; she sowed almost all the land, and when summer came she harvested the crops and took them to market in town. One morning the milkmen did not come to pick up the milk, nor had the milkers come at dawn. Furious, Old Rosa called to Arturo. Let's go, she said to him. You have to help me milk the cows and take the milk to town. The boy came down from his room, still half asleep, yawned, and then went out with his mother toward the corral. From that day on he got up with the sun, with the woman's voice, and took the milk to town. Armando, after his trip to Havana, stopped less often at the house. He came and went urgently, carrying papers, sometimes accompanied by a uniformed friend armed with gleaming pistols. Armando had hung that rusty shotgun on the dining room wall, and now he too wore a shiny pistol at his waist. Several times, Old Rosa went to the dusty weapon, took it down with great distrust, and shook her head pensively. How is it possible, she said to herself, and she hung it up on the wall again. Then she went to the altar, where the images clustered in disorderly array, and she prayed for hours. One afternoon, Arturo, when he returned from town, gave her a letter from her daughter. It said that she was finishing her studies now and was thinking of getting married. Old Rosa was disconcerted after reading the letter. How was it possible that her daughter could have decided to get married without even consulting her, without her meeting the fiancé, without her knowing what kind of family he came from and what his parents did. And his mother, she thought, is probably not a reputable woman. Immediately she wrote to Rosa, expressing her concern. At last, toward the end of December, the daughter arrived. The mother, after hugging her, welcomed her with the same words that she had used in the letter. Rosa told her not to worry, that her fiancé was very hardworking and was now finishing his studies. He may be very hardworking, said Old Rosa, but that doesn't mean he won't starve to death. The daughter burst out laughing. If he works he won't starve to death, she said. If he doesn't have a penny to his name he'll want to live off you, which means off the farm, said Old Rosa. I couldn't care less about your farm, said the daughter. He doesn't even know you have one. I haven't told him I'm from the country. Holy Mary, bellowed the mother, he doesn't know you and he thinks he's going to marry you; he must be crazy. And she continued sputtering and quarreling in a low voice. But the daughter did not reply. The next day she went to town. At the gate, Old Rosa said to her: The only thing I ask is that you don't promise to marry him until I meet him. I'm going to town next week. The daughter kissed the mother, smiled at her, and left. Old Rosa made the sign of the cross for her; she stayed there watching for a while, until her daughter reached the plain. Then she went to the well and began to draw water to sprinkle on the seed beds. For a moment, as she leaned over the well to drop the bucket, it seemed to her that on the water, next to her face, there was another face, luminous and smiling. Old Rosa looked behind her, frightened, but she saw no one. She looked up at the trees. The afternoon birds were hopping among the leaves warbling thousands of unclassifiable notes. She stood there watching them. Over the highest boughs of the ceiba tree she thought she discerned a kind of glow from a light that

ascended until it disappeared into the last leaves. It's the sun, she
said immediately; and she let the rope slip through the pulley.
The bucket touched the surface of the water, and the image of
her face shattered. Then she carefully watered all the garden
plots, pulled up the weeds that were growing among the seedlings, and broke up the heaviest clods, spreading them around
the tender shoots. And without knowing why, as she sank her
hands into the cold, damp leaves, she started to feel happy, and
suddenly began to smile, and even felt like singing. But she could
not remember the words of any song. And since she did not know
how to whistle either, she began to hum, through closed lips, a
song she was inventing at that very moment. The next day, very
early, she started to write a letter to Rosa. She told her to think
hard about what she was going to do, not to rush into marriage; in
the end she insinuated that although the fiancé did not appear to
be informed that she, her mother, had a farm, he might very well
know that she did and be hiding it until after the wedding. Don't
trust people, she told her, sometimes you think they're going to
give you their hand and they give you a fist. Her daughter did not
write back. The mother wrote to her again; and now she described how hard she had worked to raise them, the children;
how she had slaved so that she, Rosa, might study; and how she
had toiled over the land so that she, Rosa, might live in town like a
decent person, lacking nothing. But again she received no reply;
and when she asked Arturo about the girl, he replied in curt
phrases that were practically incomprehensible. She's very busy,
he would say, or sometimes, I couldn't see her today. Until
finally, having received no reply from the daughter for a month,
and having tired of Arturo's vague answers, Old Rosa decided to
go to town. I'm always telling you to find out who the fiancé is,
and you don't lift a finger, you idiot, she said to the boy that day.
So tomorrow I'm saddling the horse and going with you. You'll see
that no one fools *me* with mumbled messages. If she doesn't
answer me there's a reason, and I have a right to know what's

going on. Arturo said nothing and went up to his room. The next day, Old Rosa saddled her horse, put on her riding pants, and was all ready to go when her son came to her and said: I think it's better if you don't go to see Rosa, Mama. So you're finally going to tell me what you've all got up your sleeves, she said impatiently. The thing is that Rosa got married more than fifteen days ago, he said. Old Rosa looked fixedly at her son. She slowly went over to him, raised her hand, and smacked him across the face; immediately she hit him again on the neck and ears; in the end she checked herself, stood stock-still in front of the boy, red with fury, and said: You bastard, now you tell me—God only knows what kind of scoundrel that little fool has married. The son, facing the mother, raised a hand to touch where she had hit him, but he did not complete the movement; then he lowered his eyelids and looked at the tips of his feet. Why didn't you tell me before, said the mother; and now her words carried a slight undertone of tenderness. I just didn't dare, replied the boy. Why, said the mother. Tell me, what's going on with Rosa. The son walked over to a corner of the farmhouse, putting distance between himself and his mother. From there he said: Mama, the thing is that Rosa's husband is a Negro. Oh, God, shouted the mother, and then she screamed again, with such fury that the pigeons flew off and took refuge in the tamarind tree. Oh, God, she repeated, and pounded the floor with her feet and raised her hands to her head. And she took off running toward the kitchen. Mama, said Arturo, following her at a distance. Old Rosa went to the stove and picked up a table knife. I'm going to kill myself, she said. What an incredible disgrace, Holy Mother of God, this can't be. . . . And she continued to rant, raising the knife and pointing it at her breast, but without delivering the blow. Arturo went to her and began struggling with her, trying to take the knife away; meanwhile, the mother was beating on his back with her free hand. When Armando arrived, he separated them and confiscated the knife. Now Old Rosa was uttering

24

hoarse grunts and clutching her stomach as if she were in pain. What's going on, said Armando. Nothing, answered Arturo, it's just that she found out about Rosa. It's about time, said Armando. With all this commotion you'd think the world was coming to an end. So you knew too, the mother said to him, panting for breath. Of course I knew, said Armando; and the only reason I didn't tell you was because Arturo didn't want to upset you. What an incredible disgrace, bellowed Old Rosa. Oh, Mama, said Armando, don't be ridiculous, no one cares about these things anymore; everyone's equal now. Brute, said the mother. You talk like the son of a whore, and no son of mine. The day I'm equal to a Negro, I'll hang myself. Armando walked into the living room, stood there for a moment, and then went out to the yard. Arturo stayed with his mother for a while, trying to soothe her, but she would have none of it; she finally told him to get out and leave her alone. The boy left the kitchen. Old Rosa stood leaning over the stove, heaving violently. Oh, God, she thought, what trials you have sent me, I don't deserve these punishments. Ah, but don't think I'm going to forgive her; first thing tomorrow I'll write to her. She's not my daughter anymore. May she never set foot in this house again; may she vanish from my sight, may she starve to death. I don't want anything to do with that harlot. A Negro, she said, now in a loud voice, a Negro. It's unbelievable. What times we live in. Where will it all end. And she continued talking, raising her hands, kicking the sides of the stove, which gave off bits of ash. Until she felt (and this time with greater force) the presence of a glowing figure behind her, and heard a slight clicking sound. What the hell is going on, she said in a hoarse voice, turning her head furiously. But she was alone. And aside from the glow and the sizzling of the embers in the stove, no other noise or light was perceptible in the kitchen. The next day she wrote the letter to Rosa. She wrapped it in brown paper and gave it to Arturo as he was mounting his horse. See what happens to you if you forget to give her this note, she said to him. Don't lose it. The boy tucked the letter in his shirt pocket and went off to town. A very fine drizzle started to fall, less a drizzle than a kind of dense fog that enveloped the trees, turning them white. Old Rosa looked for a moment at the countryside covered by that whiteness, and was conscious of her damp face and her cold, wet hands. The son was already disappearing in the drizzle. For several days the fog descended and finally turned into a torrential downpour that stripped the trees and thundered down the rain gutters. Old Rosa stayed in the house during the first of the storm, walking from the living room door to the back door, where the corn shed was, watching the water fall and splatter on the yard, rising up like small clouds of smoke; but seeing that the rain was not letting up, she went out to the fields in the afternoon. She inspected all the plantings, moved the animals, and returned, when it was getting dark, with a leaf basket full of half-drowned chickens and a few bunches of bananas brought down by the wind. Through the downpour drumming on the roof, she heard the radio music; from time to time she also heard laughter. Her son appeared to be talking with a friend. In the morning it had cleared up, and all the trees glistened in the sun, and gave off a damp pleasant odor that drifted into the house, mingled with the aroma of the drenched earth. Old Rosa went out to the yard; she went to the seed bed and started to replant the seedlings that had been uprooted by the rain. The weather's getting nice again, she thought. And she went to the overflowing well, stretched out her hands, and drank the fresh water. She was still bending over when she heard women's voices in the yard. She turned and saw that the women were already at the kitchen door. Eyeing them suspiciously, Old Rosa went toward them. They had come on behalf of the manager of the cooperative and were summoning all the neighbors to a meeting. Old Rosa offered them coffee; then she asked them what kind of meeting this was that everyone had to attend. The women told her that they did not really know what the manager was going to discuss, but that he was talking of bringing all the farms in the area together in a cooperative. Old Rosa collected the empty cups and carried them to the sink. When is the meeting, she said, looking out the kitchen window toward the pine trees in the yard. Tonight, said the women; that way it doesn't interfere with production. Then they left. Armando arrived in the afternoon. He brought a great quantity of papers that he tossed on the dining room table and started to leaf through. Old Rosa approached him from behind and stood there for a while, gazing at him in silence. At last, the son turned and looked at her. Ah, he said. Lots of work, asked Old Rosa, looking at the papers. Yes, said the son. Old Rosa remained silent. Then she said: Three women came to see me today. They say I have to go to a meeting at the cooperative. And again she was silent. And she looked again at the papers that the son was inspecting, deep in thought. But I'm not going to go, she said. It's better if you go, said the son; if you want I'll go with you. You're going to be there too, asked the mother. Well, of course, I even have to speak, answered the son. At dusk, Old Rosa put on a black dress that made her sweat mercilessly, got into her good shoes that she almost never wore now, and set off with Armando. The cooperative was at the farm that had belonged to the Estradas. A wooden platform had been erected, and her son was perched up there, sitting behind a long table next to the manager, some other men, and a few women. The entire neighborhood was gathered around the platform; the peasants were talking in loud voices, arguing and laughing raucously. Old Rosa studied this scaffold that looked like a hayloft, and recognized the Pupo sisters laughing and whispering to each other behind the big table. At last, one of those men with extremely long beards began to speak. From the stream of clever words that the orator wielded, such as *welfare, exploitation, production,* and *revolution,* Old Rosa came to the *conclusion* that what he wanted was for all the peasants to turn over their land and join together in one big cooperative. As she listened to that long speech, she was looking at the Pupo sisters, and for a moment it seemed to her that they were looking at her too, and laughing. When the man with the beard finished speaking, the applause burst forth. Old Rosa looked all around her, surprised, and clenched her fists. Then Armando stood up, and he too began to speak. His words, although they did not thunder like those of the bearded one, had the same meaning. Old Rosa turned her back to the platform, bumped into a peasant who looked at her suspiciously, and set off toward the house. No one's going to trick *me,* she said, back home in no time. With great strides she crossed the main road, opened the gate to her farm, and stepped onto her land. There isn't anyone who can take this away from me, she thought as she crossed the pasture. I've broken my back for too long to let those jackasses come along now and persuade me with fancy words. Finally she arrived at her house, and stopped for an instant in the middle of the living room. Arturo, she screamed from there, turn off that damn radio. Her voice thundered so violently that for the first time the boy obeyed her and turned off the radio. Old Rosa entered the bedroom silently and threw herself on her knees before the altar. . . . The following year the crops were meager. For months, not a drop of water fell, and the cattle began to grow thin. The cows gave almost no milk, and the newly sown cornfield was drying up in the furrows. Most of the workers had taken jobs at the cooperative, abandoning the farm; only the oldest ones continued to work her land. Old Rosa got up earlier every day, drank her coffee, and went out to the fields to work; she cleared land, cut sugarcane tips for the cows that had just calved; and she even tried to divert the river with a dam and make waterways to irrigate the fields. But all her labor was not sufficient to keep up the farm. In the following months the few remaining workers went to town or decided to work on farms run by the State. Old Rosa paid her men for the last time and gave them some vegetables. They'll come back, she thought. But they did not come back. And now there was no one but her to look after everything.

Armando came by the house less and less often. Always going to meetings, the mother observed when she was alone, wasting his time on nonsense while the weeds overrun the yard and choke the crops. Arturo barely bestirred himself to go to town with what little milk the cows gave; and even this he did not do as the mother would have wished. The milk turned sour in the pitchers, and often the customers did not pay him. Finding herself alone, Old Rosa started to work at night. Her tall silhouette could be seen in the moonlight, cutting down trees, preparing the fields for sowing, leading the cows to the river. And when it was windy and there was no moon, she lit big bonfires along one side of the pasture, and illumined by their glow, she plowed the earth, contending with the oxen and prodding them furiously with the tip of the goad until dawn. But the farm did not prosper. There was still no rain. The cattle were dying of thirst. And livestock that did not belong to her squeezed through the gaps in the fences that she had not had time to mend, and ate the crops. Old Rosa continued to work tirelessly; sometimes she even forgot to eat, and there were nights when she barely slept two or three hours. She was growing thinner, and vivid blue veins started to crisscross her face and arms. Under the searing midday sun she spaded the earth in the fields, panting, occasionally raising her hands to her brow, but never stopping to rest for a single moment. In spite of everything the spring harvest was poor, and many cows starved to death tethered to the dusty fences. Old Rosa had not been able to move them anywhere else. Toward the end of June almost the entire farm was taken over by the wild pineapples, and the chinaberry tree was devoured by ants. Finally came the interminable downpours of July. With thunderbolts crashing and lightning flashing above, Old Rosa ranged over the farm from one end to the other, securing the fences, shoring up the weakest posts. Until finally she fell ill and had to take to her bed. She felt like her blood was boiling and her head was going to explode. She stayed in bed for a week, quarreling in a low voice with Arturo, who did not know how to prepare the medicinal herbs, or looking at the rafters and sensing the grass running riot, choking the flowers in the breezeway and reaching almost to the window. And she in bed, helpless. Feverish, sweating profusely, she closed her eyes and could not sleep. At a certain moment, in her delirium, she clearly saw the figure of her husband at the head of the bed. Go take care of the animals, they must be starving to death, Old Rosa said to him. Yes, Mama, answered Arturo who was at his mother's side. And he went out to the kitchen. At last, one afternoon, Old Rosa felt better and could sit up in bed. The sun was setting, and its rays filtered in through the cracks in the shuttered window. Old Rosa got to her feet and went to the kitchen. Standing next to the door, she looked at the yard. Thousands of crickets were chirping in the tall, tall grass; above the highest boughs of the laurel a flock of blackbirds swooped and screeched in a slow, constant circling. For a moment she found the commotion intolerable, and she even gestured as if to cover her ears with her hands. Then it began to get dark, and the commotion of the birds and crickets died down in the dusk. How the grass has grown, Old Rosa said to herself, and she went and sat down on the bench in the dining room. There, enveloped in the last glimmer of the afternoon, she looked, from a distance, like a forlorn little boy on the verge of bursting into inconsolable sobs. Arturo came in from the kitchen and put a cup of hot coffee in her hands. Late in the evening Armando arrived; he went to the dining room table, and by the light of the oil lamp he began, as usual, to unpack some enormous portfolios full of papers. Old Rosa, wrapped in a blanket, stationed herself behind him. How are you feeling, Mama, asked the son. She answered with a snort and went to sit down at the other end of the table, facing him. How are those cooperatives going, she said to him then, in an apparently disinterested voice. Fine, said the son, and continued to inspect his papers. A few moments later he raised his eyes, looked at his mother, and said: And you, when are you going to join them. Over my dead body, said Old Rosa. This is mine, and no one will take it away from me. The son turned to his papers again. There was a strange expression on his face, as if he were worried. But she thought it might be the effect of the light from the oil lamp, which flickered constantly. You're working too hard, said the mother. But the son did not seem to hear her, and continued to shuffle his papers laconically. Some days later a group of uniformed men arrived at the farm; they brought an array of strange instruments and started to unroll an interminable measuring tape. And Armando was with them. Old Rosa, who was near the well watering the seedlings, saw the retinue set these instruments down near the yard, and stood there motionless, curious and frightened. The men calmly continued their work; they set up an apparatus with three legs that supported a telescope, and one of them began to look through it; another walked over to the wild pineapple patch and hammered a stake into the ground. Old Rosa drew nearer, and it was then that she discovered her son. Armando, seeing her, went to her and greeted her with a nod of his head. And what's going on now, said Old Rosa. Nothing, said the son, they're surveying the farm. And who the hell authorized them to do that; how dare they set foot on my land without asking my permission, said the mother. The son tried to talk to her, but Old Rosa was already delivering a long, complicated speech punctuated by curses and threats. What the hell is this, she said. Don't they respect other people's property. If they don't show me a permit I'm going to call the police. I'm fed up with these abuses. Mama, said Armando, so violently that Old Rosa fell silent for a moment, they are the police. And you too, said the mother, and those Pupo whores, and the Negro who married my daughter; everyone is the police. But they better get the hell out of here right now if they don't want me to start shooting, and you too, you wretch. And she went to the dining room, and made as if to take down the shotgun hanging on the wall. Armando followed her slowly. Mama, he said then, they're

31

going to buy the farm from you. Old Rosa looked at her son, and standing in the middle of the room, she screamed: And who the hell told them I'm selling the farm. Mama, said Armando, you have to sell it; by law, farms over a hundred and sixty-five acres go to the State. And he finished in a low voice, as if out of respect, or fear. Suddenly, Old Rosa discovered that the dining room was expanding and emptying until it became immeasurable; and she discerned her son at a great distance, making signals with his hand, as if trying to explain something. So she drew herself up even more and prepared to scream. But an enormous glow surged over one of the corners of the dining room, and she saw, clearly now, immense wings rising above her head and disappearing beyond the rafters. I'm seeing visions, Old Rosa said then; they want to drive me crazy, but don't think it will be easy. Finally she calmed down. The glow vanished. And the dining room resumed its usual dimensions. In a dry, distant voice, Old Rosa said: My son, I have been living here for more than thirty years; you were born here, and Rosa and Arturo; my husband died here, and I'm going to die here too. And the day they force me to leave (and now she raised her voice slightly), I will take a rope and hang myself. The son came closer to the mother and tried to put his hand on her hair. She drew back; then she approached him slowly, looked at him, blinking, and smacked him across the face with both hands. Armando remained silent. And it's you, you bastard, who bring me this news, Old Rosa said to him. You, the worst bandit in the neighborhood. Mama, said the son very slowly, the Revolution . . . Old Rosa was furious. Shut your mouth, she said, interrupting him. Get out of here, you wretched thief. Dear God, what am I to do, she said now, raising her hands to the ceiling, what am I to do with a son who steals from his own mother. And looking at Armando, she pronounced her sentence: This will be your punishment. You will go to hell. Mama, the son said then, more composed, I haven't believed in God for years. Jesus, said Old Rosa, and now she was shaking. Jesus, she said again, and she left the dining room with jerky steps. The son followed her, moving slowly. The mother stopped next to the stove. She raised her eyes, this time without blinking, and in a slow, hoarse voice she asked: And when do I have to go. The son remained silent; then he looked at the flame flaring up and subsiding back into itself in the stove. You can stay here for a month, he said after a moment. In the meantime you can look for another place to live. Like two strangers, they went out to the yard and watched the men, who were jumping over the wild pineapples to stretch the tape to the farthest end of the farm. Old Rosa saw one of them trampling the tomato seedlings with his boots. She clenched her fists, but said nothing. She turned her back to her son and went to her bedroom. She stayed in front of the altar for the rest of the day, not kneeling, not saying anything, not crossing herself, only looking at the saints. At dusk, she abandoned her room and left the house. She returned at dawn. She was soaked with dew and covered with mud up to her knees. She went to bed. That day, Arturo was able to sleep all morning. At midday, the boy went to Old Rosa's room and saw her sitting on the bed. Are you sick again, he asked. I'm dead, said the mother. Do you want me to fix you some medicine, said the son. Go to hell, she answered. But Arturo did not leave the room; he went to the bed and sat down at his mother's side. What's the matter, he asked. Oh, Arturo, she said, the end of the world. And her words seemed to break, but she did not cry. When she finished speaking, the son waited a while before answering her. Finally he said: But if they pay you for the farm we can buy a house in town. We'll be better off there (and now he could no longer hide his joy); you're old now, you'll feel more at peace there. We'll buy a house across from the park. The boy went on enthusiastically with his plans. Old Rosa looked at him with an anguished expression. Not even he sympathized with her. Get out of here, she said to him then, I feel fine now. The next day, Old Rosa got up at dawn; she made coffee and called to Arturo. What is it, he said. Get up and milk the cows and take the milk to town, replied the mother. But Mama . . . , said the boy. We still have the farm, said the mother; we're still the owners, so once and for all, get up. The boy got up, grumbling. If they only had one month left, the best thing to do was spend it not working. But not wishing to oppose her, he got dressed, milked the cows, and took the milk to town. In the meantime, more diligently than ever, Old Rosa tended the cattle, cleared the woodland, and weeded the fields. Arturo noticed one afternoon, with surprise, that Old Rosa was starting seedlings for next year's crops. But he said nothing to her; he decided it was only the whims of old age. Anyway, he said to himself, it's better that she get involved in something, otherwise she might go crazy. In the afternoons, after moving all the cows and shutting the laying hens in the coop, Old Rosa saddled the horse and rode off to inspect the farm; she came to the river and stayed there quietly for a while. Then she meandered among the palm trees at the horse's slow trot. She went as far as the coconut grove, tied the horse to a tree, and threw herself to the ground. Then she abandoned herself to her worries. She made plans; she searched for a way out. She groaned. And finally, her thoughts made themselves known aloud: And yet I do have to leave, and go on living in spite of it. And her voice, loud and deep, mingled with the buzzing of the bees and the flapping of the coconut fronds. Only in the last days of the month did Old Rosa stop working. At midday she would leave for the woods, and set about improvising long, aggrieved speeches, and then she would drift off to sleep. One night she did not return to the house. The next day Arturo and two of his friends rode over the entire farm looking for her. When they were almost back at the house, they found her asleep in the tall grasses of the coconut grove, covered with dew. Mama, said the son, and Old Rosa woke up immediately; she pushed aside the spider webs and stood up. Without saying anything, she took off toward the house. The boys watched her recede from view and looked at each other, disconcerted. But when there was only one day left before they had to abandon the farm, Old Rosa got up very early, as usual, milked the cows, and sent her son to sell the milk in town. Then she went through the entire house, lingering in each corner, looking placidly at everything, down to the least nail piercing the wall. She went out to the yard and stopped next to the skyflower bush; she stretched out a hand and stroked the leaves of the plant. Then she stood at the well for a while, leaning over the edge, looking into the water at the slightly distorted reflection of her face. When night came she was walking along the edge of the wild pineapple patch. Then she went in and out of the corn shed several times, and looked at the great tall trees in the backyard. And at last she went to the porch and stood there waiting for day to come. For a moment she spread out her hands in the darkness, as if in a fleeting delirious gesture; but she immediately regained her composure. Finally, she sat down in one of the old armchairs on the porch, and watched impassively as the sky reddened and the buds on the palm trees began to glow in the sun. Dawn broke. The crowing of the roosters filled the morning. A flock of birds descended on the custard apple tree, fluttering nervously, so that it seemed the branches might break. Then, as if frightened, all the birds took flight, and gradually disappeared in a straight line along one side of the sky. It was completely light. From a distance came a sound like the noise of a truck passing by on the main road. Old Rosa opened her eyes and saw a tractor breaking up her land, making enormous furrows that obliterated the road, and suddenly it seemed to her (she felt) that this enormous iron contraption was moving back and forth now inside her chest, breaking her heart. For a long while she remained very quiet, observing it; then she saw a gray kingbird hopping around on the skyflower bush. It was already midday, and she was still sitting in the creaky old armchair. She felt the sun burning her face and the odor of dampness fading. In Arturo's room, the radio was blaring a popular song. And although she found that music intolerable, Old Rosa said nothing. She did

not even move in the armchair. The searing heat and the som-
nolent quiet came, and even the animals seemed to yawn, taking
refuge under the trees. It was then that Armando appeared. She
did not notice him until he was standing in front of her. Come in,
she said to the son, and she stood up. The two of them went to the
dining room. They sat down at the table. He gave her a paper bag
with the money for the farm. Very calmly, she began taking out
the bills, counting them, and putting them on the table. Good,
she said then, is there anything else. Yes, said the son, and he
drew a paper from his pocket and gave it to the mother. You have
to sign here. And he offered her a pen. Old Rosa read the text of
the paper laboriously; then she looked again at her son, took the
pen with clenched hand, and scrawled her name below the
writing. That's it, she said to the son, now you can get out. I'll be
leaving this afternoon. They both stood up. The son folded the
paper in silence, and the mother took the bag of money. Rigid,
like two soldiers, they stood still for a moment; then they walked
toward the living room, moving so stiffly that they seemed to be
marching, and went out on the porch. Then Old Rosa looked
toward the plain, where the midday glare was creating mirages in
the grass, and for a moment she thought she saw a kind of great
lake that rose up, shimmering, over the land. Finally, she began
to speak: Just like that, she said, this isn't mine anymore; the
worn-out hands, yes, but the land, no. And now that they're
taking what these worn-out hands made, they should also take
these hands; because now I'd like you to tell me what I'm going to
do with my hands without the land. The son tried to speak, but
she continued her discourse, waving her hands, walking to one
end of the porch, looking at the fields, talking, without a moment's pause, without waiting for replies to her interrogations,
which were no longer directed to the son, but to time, to the
trees, to no one. At last Armando, convinced that it was impossible to reason with his mother at such moments, decided to say
nothing. Then he left the house. Old Rosa went on talking in a

loud voice. And who made this, she said, if not these hands, and now you throw me out of here as if I were a thief; but you, you are the thieves, you who were nothing but a bunch of bums and drunks while I was working like an animal. And now you come to me talking about work and sacrifice. Go to hell, damn you. Talking to me about work, me who never rests. But who are they, she wondered, now talking to a different group of people; who are they but so many jealous bastards; who was sitting up on the platform that night if not the Pupo sisters, those whores, and all the local trash. And now suddenly they come and tell you you have to give up everything, as if saying that weren't the same as killing you. Oh, but of course; that's exactly what they want: they want me to die, they want me to drop dead. Lousy scum, jealous black bastards, filthy whores. And if that's the Revolution, the Revolution be damned; everything be damned. But they're wrong if they think I've given up. This hell can't go on for long. And in the meantime, don't think I'm going to starve to death. Right this second I'm leaving this godforsaken place and going somewhere else, even if it's a barren hill, but I'll never live in town. Another farm. That's what I'm going to do with the money. And start over, far away from this vermin. . . . Then she started talking in a low voice, moving her lips slowly, raising and lowering her shoulders, opening and closing the bag of money. She thinking, now silently: They're not going to drive *me* crazy. I'll buy another piece of land that's less than a hundred and sixty-five acres, and I'll start working again. And she immediately began to collect her clothing. And again she inspected the entire house; the furniture, the corn shed, the cabinet crammed full of broken plates that she had not thrown out. Just then the radio music resounded very clearly through the house. At least Arturo's with me, thought Old Rosa; I'll go get him right now to help with the packing. And hearing that music, which she suddenly did not find so intolerable, she started to climb the stairs that led to her son's bedroom. She climbed slowly. Wearily. Stopping sometimes on a step to catch her breath. The radio was now playing some very soft music that at the moment was almost a comfort to her. Without knowing why, before opening the door, she stood there listening to the music. Then she heard, mingled with the notes, the sounds of a conversation. Arturo seemed to be talking with another person. But who the devil, thought Old Rosa; who could have gone up to her son's bedroom. It was impossible, for she had been in the house all day and had not seen any of the boy's friends arrive. Perhaps he was talking to himself. She held her breath and came closer to the door. Although it was very difficult to understand the words that reached her, Old Rosa deduced that the boy was not alone. His voice was very hoarse, and occasionally it seemed to rise, trembling. Then the words became comprehensible. But they were only isolated words that were even more disconcerting. She tried to concentrate harder, and for a moment she thought the son was praying, but now and then someone answered him. Yes, the other voice was saying; and then only the radio music was audible. More and more intrigued, Old Rosa stood for an instant leaning against the door, uncertain whether to open it. And although at that moment she could not explain why, an obscure sensation of terror was settling into one of the most indeterminate regions of her body. Hardly daring to breathe, she started to open the door. And she peeked inside. The two boys, almost naked, were standing in the middle of the room, kissing. Then they fell, as one body, onto the bed. Old Rosa closed the door again, very slowly. She descended the stairs, crossed the living room, and without stopping, went to the dining room wall and took down the dusty shotgun. With the weapon clutched in her hands, she set off again toward the bedroom. She went slowly, climbing the stairs with an almost martial gait, without stopping once to rest. Again she arrived at the door of the room and cautiously opened it halfway. The two figures were still embracing on the bed, and the radio was playing the soft music that she had not minded. With great precision, she raised the gun to her shoulder and fired. The first shot resounded in that close room, passed over the boys, and lodged in the radio, which shattered into pieces. The boys, terrified, jumped up and looked at Old Rosa, who was aiming at them again. They ran to the window, forced it open, and leaped out. With a loud crash they fell into the garden and took off running, pulling up their pants. Old Rosa went to the window and fired again. The shot hit the withers of the old horse that was grazing impassively near the crown-of-thorns plants. The horse reared up, uttered a death whinny, and fell into the bed of yellow irises, kicking violently. Old Rosa, almost choking, squeezed the trigger again. The shotgun produced a deafening explosion and disintegrated in her hands. The boys were already disappearing, leaping over the wild pineapples at the edge of the woodland. Old Rosa looked at the worthless shotgun at her feet, and went back down the stairs. She crossed the living room again, entered her bedroom, and stood there, rigid, looking at the altar. God, she said. God. . . . And she did not pray, and she did not kneel. She was not there to beg, but to ask for an accounting, to demand an explanation. For how is it possible, she said to herself, that these things are happening to me. How can You let me suffer such disgrace. Haven't I been faithful to You; haven't I prayed to You day after day; haven't I begged You and gotten down on my knees here every afternoon, for hours on end, until my knees are raw and the blood freezes in my legs. Don't You hear me. Or have all my prayers been worth nothing. Or don't You exist. And she raised her voice dramatically. And then she was silent for a moment, expectant. But she only heard the commotion of the afternoon as the sun disappeared behind the trees. Then she raised her arms threateningly and approached the images on the altar. And again she felt the dazzling of an intolerable radiance at her back. And this time, when she turned, dazed, with a gesture of fury, her eyes met the resplendent figure of an angel. It was there in the bedroom, on one side of the bed: the enormous feathery wings brushing the ceiling; the luminous silhouette blinking in the room; the arms lightly spread as in a gesture of mercy; the feet naked and rosy, the toes barely touching the floor; the intense clear eyes, blinking lightly as the long lashes rose and fell in a rhythmic fluttering; and the radiant face displaying an unfathomable smile. Old Rosa looked at it, frightened; then she retreated to one side of the altar. She remained there for a moment, looking at the angel, who was still smiling. And then a hatred more enormous than all the passions she had ever conceived was unleashed upon that resplendent figure. Something told her that the angel was her worst enemy. For it was the angel who had appeared at her back at every terrible moment, and not exactly to help her; since it began appearing, her misfortunes had grown greater all the time. And now, now that I don't know how I'm going to go on living, you show yourself at last, smiling and mocking my tragedy. And she remembered, with desolate clarity how that glow had followed her day after day as things got worse and worse. And then in the last months, she had been feeling that presence at every moment, shadowing her everywhere; until finally, when the misfortunes reached their peak and continued to abound, the angel's presence had almost become her own; and as she was experiencing this revelation, she saw the angel among the pots and pans in the kitchen; next to the table, at mealtime; at the mouth of the well when she drew water for the garden; among the ceiling rafters when she threw herself into bed longing for sleep. And now, now that the misfortunes were reaching their limit and transporting her to a timeless region where the defeats did not even have meaning, this figure of ill omen was there, clearer than ever, unmistakably mocking her tragedy. For if you are good, it makes no sense that you come to console me when all is lost, when it was your duty to prevent these misfortunes; but no, you prevented nothing, instead you came to haunt me every time something bad happened, so what can you be but the Devil himself come to laugh at me in my disgrace. And as she said these words, she felt that she had been swindled all her life. And she touched the dimensions of an immeasurable solitude that would be her lot from this day forward. But you're not the Devil, she said finally, and now her words seemed to stumble upon the terrifying answer. You are something worse. You are nothing. And she took one of the plaster figures and hurled it furiously at the angel's head. The image shattered, and the angel went on smiling imperturbably. Then Old Rosa started hurling all the altar figures at the angel. The virgins whistled through the air and smashed against the glowing wings, the neck, the long, fluttering lashes; at times they collided with its extended hands and flew over the bed in a thousand pieces. Damn you, Old Rosa said, and she threw the altar boards at it, the enormous candles, the heavy medallions hanging on the wall. But the angel went on smiling imperturbably. And suddenly Old Rosa thought she saw that smile spreading, becoming a grotesque cackle that echoed through the entire house. Infuriated, Old Rosa hurled the lamps at it, the pictures on the wall, the calendars; the living room furniture sailed through the air and smashed against the resplendent figure. Old Rosa heard the cackle echoing more and more loudly. And then it no longer seemed to her that it was coming only from the angel, but from everywhere, from the house, from the trees, and even from her own body. I'll kill you, you bastard, she said, raising her voice to such a pitch that she heard herself above the deafening cackles. And she ran through the house, went to the corn shed, and there snatched up two dried palm fronds. She carried them to the stove and set them on fire at both ends. And while she was waiting for the flames to catch in those parched leaves, she felt, suddenly, that she was turning into an old woman; and all the ravages that time had wrought she discovered now, with an indefinable terror. Almost painfully then, she felt her face blossoming with wrinkles that spread like lightning down her neck and wove a spider's web around her eyes, consumed her lips and descended to her arms and hands. And when she crossed the kitchen, wielding the two torches, she saw her figure reflected in the depths of one of the brass pots hanging on the wall. She was an old woman. But she did not have time to meditate upon this tragedy, which her affairs had not allowed her to discover until this moment. She ran through the house and entered her bedroom. I'm going to roast you, she said to the angel; it was still glowing, and now its cackles seemed to soar. And for a moment (which not even she herself could pinpoint) she thought she saw that figure of radiant youth raise one of its delicate hands to the region of the body where men flaunted their virility. And suddenly she remembered with terror that her husband had once made that very same gesture. And a new fury possessed her. And she raised the two palm fronds and thrust them at the angel, and she saw it laughing, its hand placed over *that accursed region.* Then Old Rosa went about setting fire to the entire bedroom, torching the mattress, the planks that had been the altar. She gazed at the angel, and it was still glowing and smiling, but surrounded now by fire. You won't escape from here, Old Rosa said to it, and she watched the door, transformed into a great blaze, come down in a grinding of hinges. She went out to the living room, holding the two torches; she quickly set fire to the cabinet, the doors, and the eaves of the roof. Then she went to the back and set the corn shed ablaze. She returned, practically walking over the red-hot coals; she went to the living room, where the flames were already leaping onto the porch, illuminating the whole garden. Cockroaches were running across the floor; the old bats that slept hanging from the ridgepole flew about blindly as the roof supports started to totter. Old Rosa closed her eyes for a moment and felt the crackling grow more and more intense; the flames were exploding in front of her body, which was once more making its way back to the bedroom. There she gazed at the angel again, and it was still smiling, though the smoke and the strength of the fire had diminished its splendor. Old Rosa observed it in silence. At that moment, a roofbeam exploded over her head, singeing her hair. She brushed the sparks off with her hands and went to the living room, which was already ablaze. She stood there for a second, watching the fire consume the walls and begin to leap through the windows. In the end she went out to the yard, almost enveloped in flames, leaned against the tamarind tree that no longer flowered, and began to cry in such a way that the tears seemed never to have begun, but to have been there always, flooding her eyes, producing that creaking noise, like the noise of the house at the moment when the flames made the strongest posts totter, for now the house was no more than a swaying flash of fire that threatened to crash down at any moment. When night fell, the whole farm was bright with flames. The wild pineapples were vanishing in a long wake of fire; the crops and the oldest trees exploded in the wind, in a crackling of leaves and scorched birds. The flames continued to rise around Old Rosa, who went on crying in a measured and monotonous flow. There she was, her breath coming in hoarse rattles, when she felt a brilliance at her back that did not come from the flames. She did not even have to turn to know that it was the angel, that figure of radiant youth, smiling, its hands still extended. Old Rosa went on crying; and only when the smoke was filling her throat, almost asphyxiating her, and the flames were burning her hands, did she stop crying, and she moved back until she stumbled against the angel's legs. And so she remained, without protesting, without looking at the angel, feeling those cool legs against her back. Finally, she huddled even closer until she was completely enfolded in that body. Then the flames rose up, stirred by the midnight breeze, and the tamarind tree shriveled, swept by a luminous explosion. Old Rosa could see the fire devouring her dress. And feeling that she could no longer stand, she tried to lean into the angel even more. But it was useless: the angel too was burning. Yet, for a moment, they remained motionless. Then the fire began to consume the two figures, which no longer were distinguishable.

Havana, 1966

The Brightest
Star

TRANSLATED FROM THE SPANISH

BY

Andrew Hurley

For Nelson,
in the air

"I HAVE SEEN A LAND OF REGAL ELEPHANTS, FAR, FAR away," he had written some years ago, not many really, when he was still convinced that a cluster of signs, a cadence of images perfectly described—*words*—might save him . . . and now, he brought those elephants down and slowly, carefully set them, the wondrous, peaceable, palpable figures, at the end of the broad plain on which his great work was at last beginning to take shape; for though no one could deny that he had exerted himself up to now, though for a very long time he had not wasted a single free moment, devoting himself entirely to the infinitely patient construction of an enormous, enormous tree, a stone, a jewel of shifting hues, an expanse of water with no guards posted at its shore, a human face, still it was only now, really, at last, that those efforts were beginning to take on a supreme coherence, were tending toward a perfect, orderly, rare, grand, and grandiose conclusion; and his ideas were mysteriously falling into place now in just that way—they came to him and he selected, he picked and chose among them, rejecting those images too simple or too trite, too often used, too ugly or too sad, those which he faced or had to contemplate every single day and which without a doubt they, the others, the rest, all of them, were hurling at him, pitching at him, throwing in his way, into his memory (or his dreams), to screw around with him, out of spite, to *screw* him, always screwing him, trying to ruin his work, spoil it, interrupting him, trying to confuse him, throw him off, make him lose his way, break his concentration, and to shrink him, too, cut him down to size, make him fit their stupid frames of thought, the meanness of their vision, the world, *their* world (the world of *them*), fit, conform to life, or *their* repulsive lives; but all his thought now, all his strength, and strength of will, and even his gestures, his entire organism and its desires, and all its senses, were taut, clean, clear, alert, and ready—set to take in or reject, and if they took in, to transfigure, even to sacrifice, if need be, on behalf of the glorious masterwork that was flowing through them; and now he felt that stinging again, again that burning never felt before yet somehow familiar, though he couldn't say why—a tingling, a sense of growth and power, a burgeoning, as though something were lifting him up, raising him, as though he were floating (once more, once more), and in this rarefied space he went up, and up, and up, guided, liberated, by the impulses of his genius, his genie, which in his eyes had taken on such dimensions, such virtuosity, that it was as though it had declared its independence from the rest of his being, from the physical organism, the dross, and from the instruments necessary for its expression, even from his brain; it was as though someone—he himself yet not he—were performing, playing some inconceivable role, making gestures never seen before, evoking tears, joy, fullness of heart, casting before an audience outside time a rhythm, a song, the one and only, most exquisite music, the melody all the world had dreamed of, had secretly been waiting for in fear and joyous longing, and now at last he was seeing himself bestow those wonders on the world, he was seeing *him* . . . but suddenly he had a chill akin to terror to think that on the other hand he might be only an instrument, a mere tool, an artifact, and that the glorious melody, the grand creation, the work, was rising, would rise, of its own accord, was simply there, ineluctable, inexorable, and that it was only using him, as it might have used any other man, and as it used its interpreters as well, the passive, the vicarious ones, those who only looked, heard, contemplated, so that it (the work) might take its place, manifest itself, and bear witness, from time to time, to an unvarying, impregnable, unyielding eternity, availing itself now, at this very moment, of a simple, ignorant, humble messenger, a messenger that overwhelming horror, and of course chance, too, had determined would be he . . . and he secretly felt that even at this most sublime moment of his existence, the moment that gave his whole life meaning, even then, even now, he was still, and always, the victim of a swindle, a double-cross, a trick—that he was a slave; and yet, couldn't it be *them,* with that typical malevolent persistence of theirs (that sole authentically human persistence), who kept doggedly hammering such mad thoughts into his brain? them, with their endless, stupid conversations, with their exaggerated, effeminate, affected, artificial, false, gross, grotesque gesturings and posturings, pulling everything down to their own level, deflating, discounting everything, cheapening and corrupting everything, even the authentic rage of the man who suffers terror, even the brutal ritual of kicks, rifle butts against flesh, slaps in the face? for even the firing squad had been transformed by them, turned into a flurry of arcane words, a burlesque show of clichéd attitudes and wisecracks, a joke; them, whittling the tragedy down to size, the eternal tragedy of submission, of their own eternal disgrace and misfortune, jeering at it, making bitchy fun of it, shrinking it to the simple stridency of bedlam—shrill laughter, the rhythmic fluttering of batted eyelashes, a moue, a hand held limp like a broken wing, the vulgar parody of some classical dance; them, painting their faces with whatever came to hand, weaving wigs from strips of palm fronds and agave fibers, sewing miniskirts out of burlap

sacks sneaked from the guarded storerooms, and at night parad-
ing their dissatisfactions, shrieking, making a show of their
stupid slang, their stupid exhibitionist moves and motions, their
wiggles and giggles and languid wrists, their masks, which so
long worn had become their own, true faces . . . and who among
them, who there, even for a few fleeting moments, stopped, and
thought? who ever seized the chance, rarer every day, to run,
flee, escape? . . . so it was thanks, then, to them ("the sister-
hood," as they insisted), it was their own fault that he had chosen
to be, to act, to grow superior, although it might have been the
others, the ones that came after them (he had established three
categories: *them, the others,* and *the rest*), the ones that guarded,
the ones that considered themselves superior, the elect, the pure,
the high and mighty ones who prided themselves on never having
had, never having (though it wasn't necessarily true), relations
with anybody but women, babes with big tits, chicks, foxes, *this
big, I'm tellin' ya, this big,* women with suppurating orifices,
cunts, which when penetrated (and when they crowed about it in
public) lent them, and the rest as well (all of them, to a man,
incorrigible braggarts), a kind of acclaim, a vote of confidence, a
higher position, the privilege to step on and insult; yes, now that
he thought of it, it might have been the others, actually, the
superior ones, the ones in uniform, in command for the moment,
the ones with the weapons, but with the same slang (or if
different, equally disgusting and detestable), with the green
trucks and jeeps, green cars, green buses, and green motorcy-
cles, the same green as their clothes, they might have been part of
it too, the top bananas, the bosses, or worse, the bosses' deputies
and dupes, the violent ones that scratched their crotches and
yelled, "Run, you faggots!"—maybe those were the ones that had
forced, impelled, virtually ordered him to choose to become
superior, God; and then too, there was the futility of all his
previous efforts, of all the useless, hopeless, desperate artifices
he had employed in order to survive, which had sharpened his

powers of selection, his sense of smell, his animal fear, but anyway, however it was, he knew that now, right now, there could be no doubt about it, the moment of the glorious unification had arrived, the true coming together, and all the oppression, exhaustion, and senselessness of an existence superficial in the first place, enslaved in the second, futile always, all the dull pain of that life, was disappearing, quite simply fading away into the grand esplanade on which he had just placed the stately elephants, and where now he conjured up a rose garden, because (he told himself, or intuited, as he added a twig for balance here, deepened the green of a mass of foliage there, invented an utterly new color over there) reality lies not in the terror one feels and suffers but in the creations that overpower that terror, and wipe it out, for those creations are stronger, realer, truer than the terror . . . and since there was still nobody there, nobody came for him, nobody had discovered him yet, since he couldn't hear the fairies' voices in the cells or in the barracks or in the work camp, those affected voices always tattling, carrying tales, calling out, trying to keep him from putting the last touches on some wonderful, urgent piece of work—an unrepeatable parasol, some utterly unique nook—no, since the soldiers hadn't started looking for him yet either, since nobody was there, he might have time, he thought, he might actually have the time (though always, in the past, someone, some intruder—never *him*, the man he was waiting for—had butted in before he could finish the row of windows gleaming in the sun, or touch the waters of a river with green and gold and silver), it looked like this time, today, he had chosen the right spot, he'd actually managed to escape, to slip away without their seeing him, had gotten past the guard and everyone else, gotten away from the camp and found a place and made a nest, not like before—too little distance and too little time—but far away and all alone, independent, or all alone at least till *he,* the exquisite one, arrived, alone just till the glorious construction was completed and *he,* the exquisite one, came to stay at last; yes,

it looked like he'd chosen his site well, and at least for the time
being there was no way for them, or the others, or the rest, either
(the ones in that other hell, in towns and cities, dressed in
civilian clothes, walking along the well-patrolled sidewalks like
cattle, fearfully, timidly, and almost gratefully, the great majority
of them), no way for any of them to come and bother him, so that
he actually had time, so much time that had he wanted to, Arturo
could probably have afforded himself the biblical luxury of a rest
before going on with his magnificent creation . . . but in fact, he
decided, there was no time to waste, so over there, over by the
elephants, he caused wondrous columns to spring up, columns
that would support hanging gardens, elevated terraces where he
and *he* would be able to stroll . . . and farther off, a little path
bordered by yellow-flowered grasses opens onto the sand, and
then there is the ocean, the ocean and the beach, which will be
connected to the castle by tiled, dank tunnels and secret passageways, and next, after that, some high trails overgrown by a
perennial profusion of flowers—and as he built on that sand the
steep staircase that would lead to the watchtowers in the castle's
outlying walls, Arturo smiled . . . at first everything had been so
horrible, everything was so bright and grotesque, so obviously
unbearable—the relationships with the interned fags ("fags just
like *you*," they screamed at him), mealtimes, the terrifying bath-
times, the work in the sun, the endless, endless days in the
canefield chopping, while at the far end of the access road to the
field, the soldier stood impassive, sober, self-assured, superior,
planted there stiff and straight, to all appearances for all eternity,
and eternally watching, always watching, keeping his eyes fixed
on him, on Arturo, and slowly scratching his balls, in homage to
him, to Arturo, and Arturo, soaked with sweat, eternally chopping, raising his machete and letting it fall, his feet stirring
whirlwinds of fire with every step, making the dry cane leaves
crunch, crack, creak, Arturo would look up and steal a glance at
that strong, impassive figure planted firmly there, the figure that

kept on, kept on, as though unconsciously, as though instinctively, as though for no one, really, as though with no real reason
or intention, kept on scratching his balls, making that inescapable, undeniable gesture, and Arturo's feet in a whirlwind,
crunching, the sun overhead beating down, making the canefield
shimmer, the dry harsh chop of his blade, all the blades, all
across the field, chopping, chopping, as the sweat poured down
his body—back then, at first, through all that, Arturo had tried
to devote himself solely, fully, to that crunching, to those dry
chopping sounds in the sun, to the long disquisitions about
whether the water truck would come today or not, and to the
fixed stare, the irresistible gesture of that soldier, oh, how he had
tried to become, *be,* like them, be just a tame beast that turned
ferocious over the most insignificant things, how he had tried to
become a creature without memory, without desire for even the
most important things (what is, what was, really important
anymore?), be a creature dully inhabiting a superficial, threatening present (passing, and passing him by)—but no matter how
diligently he applied himself to these hells, there always came to
him, out of the din of spoons and tin plates, or exploding in the
glare and the swaying of the cane stalks, the soft, insistent,
rhythmic murmur, the barest whisper of a ceiba tree, the ceiba
tree, and that sea . . . or other times, as he scrabbled in the dirt to
pull up a crooked stalk of sugarcane, it might be cherry blossoms
that Arturo smelled, there, in springtime, the perfume lightly
brushing his face; or dewdrops, or the shine of the leaves, or
sometimes a tiny insect with a purple shell and truly astounding
violet antennas might transport him, float him away and deposit
him in that place where all his memories seemed to flow together
and diverge again, where all scents, all sounds, all the bodies he
had smelled, heard, tasted, enjoyed, became real again, where in
fact everything that once had been just another common, ordinary, everyday smell or sound or body, a natural act unconsciously performed, sometimes almost with ennui, was now

haloed by a splendor, a grace, a beauty, a charm that distance only
served to nurture and enlarge . . . but there was no exit, there
was really no way out, and however hard he tried to change, to
accept, to conform, to just *be* there, here, in this new hell—
behind an empty tank, behind a cane cart, on the road where the
heat made glaring mirages, at the edge of a swamp—in the
distance he always thought he could see the end of a wide
breezeway, and mornings, when he awoke, he always confused
the gibberish of the barracks cooks with the unmistakable voice
of his mother; but he kept applying himself to his work, he went
into the bathroom like everybody else at the regulation time, he
parodied the absurd lyrics of the popular songs they all sang, and
in the barracks, when it was time to let your hair down and wail,
or shout, or shriek, like *thiiiiis,* in a high soprano falsetto, God,
he was the one who shrieked the loudest, and when it was time
for the "fashion show" at those forbidden parties (which were in
fact always discovered by the soldiers, who participated in them
as the most enthusiastic spectators), it was he, Arturo, who
always wore the shortest skirt now, who made himself up most
outrageously, who sported the most outlandish wig, and in the
grand finale sang the most scandalous song, rhymed by him on
the spur of the moment, its patently obscene meaning made more
obscene by movements and gestures, winks and fluttering eyelashes, glances and provocative looks—and after the party, the
same soldier who watched him chopping all day would make that
same gesture, and the two of them would go out into the canefield, where Arturo would painstakingly dedicate himself to producing pleasure, yet even when he felt the violence and the
delight of that body spending itself on his body, in his memory
the vine in the breezeway, the shimmering colors of the flowers in
the strong evening sun, and even their perfume, the sweet scent
of millions of flowers creeping up over the roof of the house, those
pictures refused to be clouded over with this *now* . . . there was a
funeral, there was a funeral, and he, Arturo, dressed all in

white, was walking at the head of the procession, he alone, in front, just behind the black hearse that thanks to his brother Armando's influence had come all the way to that backwater . . . and now he was remembering, he remembered all of it in minute detail, in such detail that it was realer than the moment itself, because the event was no longer polluted by the moment's insistence, or by his immaturity, his exhibitionism—all in white, all in white—no, now, in memory, it was the event evoked pure, suffered anew, free of the dregs, so he could walk (forever?) behind that gleaming black contraption bearing the singed remains, that forked charcoal *thing*, the burned body of the only person who had ever loved him, loved him so much that she would have killed him had it not been for an error in calculation and the decrepitude of the firearm; the hearse rolled on, and he was walking behind it, serious, sad, ridiculous, and yet lucid enough to know (for his sadness made him see) that this was hell he was living in, and that hell was all there was; but even then, even then, there were still the trees, some small refuge, and other people, and later the being alone, enjoying the solitude, even if he already knew, already knew . . . the soldier, like always, finished with a deep sigh, almost a grunt, and, like always, pulling his body away, he said, Wait, stay here till I get back to camp . . . parks, there had to be parks, big shady parks rolling away to the horizon, parks where the evening sun would throw the thin, graceful outlines of palm trees across the lawns, to shatter in fountains whose liquid jets would make shifting clouds of spray so tenuous and misty that at a distance you might glimpse any yearned-for, longed-after figure at all, parks dotted with beds of flowers, fragrant mounds and hillocks, paths leading, for all anyone knew, nowhere at all, gigantic trees with aerial roots knit into a wide roof under which *he,* the other, would surely stop and wait for him, parks with coves, nooks, byways, a lovely bench and a drooping tree for evenings when, for balance, a touch of melancholy was needed, and as he thought *parks, parks, parks,* the esplanade was filled with those whispering, murmuring, green-and-silvery shining retreats . . . and still the hearse rolled slowly on, and he walked behind it, and his brother and sister behind him (and then, farther back, the few campesinos who had dared walk with Old Lady Rosa to her final rest); and as soon as they got back they moved out of the settlement, with Armando laying out the plan for Arturo's move to town, his lodging in a decent place, his life now and in the future, and all of it without looking at him, with an air of superiority and indifference, or of contempt, or of disgust; Rosa had hugged him several times, but it hadn't been Arturo she was embracing, it hadn't been for being himself, Arturo, that he'd been embraced, but just because at the moment he was handy and she could justifiably hug him; and Armando soon drifted away to his cooperatives, and El Negro, as everybody called Rosa's husband, looked so angry and seemed to be trying to dodge them—especially the offended, accusatory looks of the campesinos—so Arturo let his sister press his head to the hollow of her neck, call him by name and cry over him, let his brother take him to a "Family Boarding House" (as its sign said), and give him some money, and enroll him in school, and order him around and belittle him, though honestly, at first, at that moment, the shock of the change had been so great that Arturo was really not fully conscious of it all; at first, just like here, just like now, it wasn't the sound of cars or trucks that woke him, but the squeak of the pulley as she, Old Rosa, drew water down there at the well, but little by little he discovered that it's easy to fit in anywhere, slip into any reality at all, as long as you don't take it seriously, as long as you secretly scorn it, look down your nose at it, despise it, and that there's always a way to lose yourself, to get lost . . . a Christmas tree, one of those wonderful big pine trees that only grow in regions he would never ever see, in climates made (so he thought) for speaking and strolling slowly, in climates created (so he thought) for smiling, not for sweating, in those glorious climates where (of this he was absolutely sure) noble, beautiful things sprouted and grew in endless cyclical profusion—this giant fir, of silky needles, rose tall and erect on the lawn, where soon, one day, he and *he* would decorate its branches and dance under its evergreen boughs . . . his first refuge, his first escape, had been libraries, which was no doubt why his first consolation, the first stratagem he'd discovered, had been words; he would walk in a kind of ecstasy down the aisles lined with shelves full of books, stretch out a hand, and take a volume down; and no reading ever surpassed that moment, the sheer pleasure of that moment, the happiness, the mystery of the moment when his hand touched the book chosen yet still unopened; but little by little he grew accustomed to, became part of that new environment, he merged with it, he let himself be carried along by it; in the music room of the library there was a group of young gay men, always on the alert, and the moment they caught sight of him they wanted to capture him, conquer him, and though Arturo at first resisted, dodging, hiding, taking refuge in the stacks, or playing that he was startled and slipping away, still somebody, something over and above his outward manner, over and above his defenses, his flights, somebody, or something, betrayed him, or perhaps it simply came to be what he truly was: like them, like them ("like *them*, nothing—like *us*," they told him), and inevitably, he lived like they lived: long predawn hours, through the least frequented parts of the city, they came at last to the ruins; for of course there were still cabarets, cafés, coffee shops, the occasional party back then, even Carnival one year, but Arturo noticed that they all spoke in the past tense, and in that whirlwind of inconclusive adventures, inconclusive conversations, inconclusive encounters and relationships, what perhaps most surprised him (perhaps even fascinated him) was to see how quickly everything, even the streets, even faces, even the weather, deteriorated, cracked, broke, eroded, day after day, from bad to worse to unbearable—one week it was a boarded-up movie theater, the next yet another item rationed, the next a business shut down, no reason given, and in a single day every tree on the street cut down, certainly no reason given *this* time, no one warned, and then the brightness, the glare that set in, just as the water service began to fail, and the glare more glaring every day—had that horrible light always come through his bedroom window like that before? had there always been that blindingly bright sky, that sun slapping you in the face, those tortured noons? before, at first, not so long ago, hadn't the afternoons been slower, easier to breathe in? had we always suffocated? and hadn't people been quieter then, more still? hadn't we sometimes had evening, twilight?—something was rotting, something had definitely gone bad and was going rotten—something? everything! everything was rotting, there was something in the countless futile mornings, yes, now back in his room after some furtive, quick, and incomplete tryst at the entrance to a stairway, or in a risky portico or vestibule, or in the bathroom of an apparently deserted tenement, something that told him that everything was rotting, becoming refuse and rubbish, your life too, your youth, yours and everybody's, everything—and the glare, God, even in darkness, and the fear that grew and grew and grew . . . but his mother, tall, stern, firm, was there, watching from the shade, the little shade there was, ordering, nagging, helping him undress, his mother folding back the sheets, rocking him? crooning to him? like she'd never done before, like never before—was she? or not? was she?—and he would drop off to sleep, at last, with the sense of her there in the room . . . but shouldn't there be levees? or big, solid earthworks, great dams along one side of his vast domain? high dams with airy walkways along the top, and guard rails on which, arms entwined, the two of them, he and *he,* would lean, and peer into the chasm below—dams, and deep blue-green waves beating against them forever; and so off to one side of the wide esplanade he raised those massive dams, and softly flowing waters cascaded down their sides in serene falls, over wide verges where glorious,

lush white flowers grew, cupped like upside-down parasols . . .
and that night, or a night long before, or "one night," anyway,
there was a concert, and it was, miraculously, advertised (no
doubt because the pianist was Russian), so by afternoon all the
fairies were already readying their finery, Arturo too participat-
ing in those ceremonies, and a half-hour before the performance
was to begin, they filed into the theater, where Arturo saw,
probably for the first time, the firm, broad shoulders of confi-
dent, well-placed young men, shoulders so different from those
of the crowd he was with, from his own, for that matter, backs,
bodies, hands simply and firmly carried, at the service of a self-
assurance, a tradition, a law that excluded him, them, and the
young men's women too, with their white white faces, almost
sweet, almost candylike, almost unheard of in these climes, and
all those people seemed to glide, flow, under the discreet lights
glowing in the gilded ceiling-sky; they took their seats quietly, as
though they had undergone some transformation, and the lights
dimmed, and the flutterings of Arturo's friends grew still, and
the curtains opened on the orchestra and its conductor; and then
the music began to fill the theater, and all of space and time was
flooded with the sound, and ennobled by it, the audience was
mantled in a rare and wonderful spell, their hands were brushed
by warmth, they felt the music flow over, through, their bodies,
and lift them, and Arturo felt himself rising, being carried away,
to a place, another place, not this; the music softly cradled
Arturo, picked him up, lifted him out of his seat, and gently,
drawing back the draperies, set him down beside a tower, in a
flowerbed, in the afternoon, next to the chinaberry tree and the
blossoming dog-rose bush by the breezeway, *the music* . . . Arturo
had watched his mother aim the gun straight at his chest, perfectly sure of what she was doing, and he hadn't cried; he had
been abandoned in the middle of the woods by his terrified
friend, and he'd gone back to the house and found nothing but
ashes and his mother's blackened body, and he hadn't cried; and

he had, he had felt the contempt (the indifference) of his brother
and sister, the contempt and indifference of all the people he had
to greet, whether he wanted to or not, and he had suffered the
torments of tawdry rooms in boardinghouses, and then the desperation and the desires, after a futile night of wandering
through the city, and he had had the hopeless (precocious),
utterly lucid realization that soon he would start to grow old, and
that the best part of his youth was lost, and he had had the vision,
terrifying in its clarity, that if the world in general was terrible,
for him it was even worse—a strait, strict, narrow, suffocating
prison growing narrower every day, a monstrous fraud, a black
joke, an unabating terror—and he hadn't cried, no, he hadn't
cried; but now, here, in the middle of this rapt gentle crowd—
him floating, listening—suddenly, out of nowhere, the tears
began to flow, to roll down his cheeks, and he could feel that his
face was bathed in tears, and he felt too, he knew, that he
couldn't stop them, that there was nothing he could do to keep
them back, but he also felt, he knew, that he was almost happy—
sheaves, byways, the mottled leaves of caladiums, a cockatoo,
coffered ceilings, and standing before a motionless sea a man
bleeding to death in the snow, and him saving him . . . because he
made snow too, that clean soft limpid snow so often dreamt of,
never seen, so many times so badly copied with cotton balls and
mirrors and ashes, but now, suddenly, there, right there on the
esplanade, clean, soft, and *palpable,* snow—snow to slide on,
sled down, roll over and over in, make snow angels in, snow so
white, so white snow-white that it would reflect their figures
back to them, snow with its infinite hints and suggestions, its
varied, impossible comforts and protections, *the music,* the music
and him strolling along beside a beautifully crafted, high, strong
railing of fine balusters, *the music,* the music and him exploring
the deepest and most secret whorls of the enormous water lilies,
lotuses floating on enormous lily ponds, there, over there, just
beyond the grove, *the music,* the music and his tears, flowing,

flowing—for it was only now, too, that he realized the extent of his grief, now when he saw that cinder-black body, the house, irrecoverable, atomizing, scattering to the winds, blowing away in a whirlwind, the tall tower he'd built, and there was the peace, too, but it was now that he could finally feel, almost physically touch with his fingertips, the timeless dimensions of his fixed and unalterable solitude, or maybe not fixed and unalterable but changing, yet changing only to take on still larger and more grotesque proportions, *the music,* the music transporting him to far-off places, translating, exalting into great and grand events things that when they had happened (if they had ever happened) were nothing but common, ordinary, everyday, vulgar things that happened, *the music,* and everything so distant and so noble, everything so heartbreakingly irrecoverable, so lost, *the music,* the road down through tall dusty trees, the house, the gentleness, the peacefulness, the softness, now, of the landscape, the fire against the sky, a little castle, a flock of birds gliding to the moon where the giant would eat them up, and gliding along with them the mother, his mother, gigantic, unique, sputtering out sparks, waving her arms like wings, already growing smaller and smaller and smaller . . . there was his mother now, standing just outside the breezeway, between the flowerbeds and the prickly crown-of-thorns plants growing wild, waiting for him; and the two of them, as they did almost every afternoon, going out to ride over the land, their land; there was that one day when night surprised them still far out on the other side of the pasture, but they went down to the river, watered the horses, and then rode back up again, and neither one of them dismounted, not once, Arturo listening to his mother talk, talk to him, to nobody, to the stars, or about the stars, yes, about the position of the stars, whether it looked like rain or a long dry spell, whether they ought to plant—*and of all of them the brightest one is that one,* she was saying, this tall figure whose silhouette by now was one with the horse, and she pointed to the lucifer-looking spark sputtering just over the hilltops, and they both sat there unmoving, watching the twinkling gleams, and then Old Rosa, Old Lady Rosa, like always, said flatly and inarguably, *Let's go to the house,* and she clucked at the horse and kicked once; her son, behind her, followed, *the music,* and she, that tall figure, pointing, *the music,* and she, the protector-figure, that loved and loving figure, for him the only figure honestly and truly venerable, saying, *Look,* and at crowded, stinking, shrill bus stops, in the dusty little towns of the island through which he'd passed in a crowded, stinking, suffocating bus—that was the way every trip anywhere was—with an eye always on the crotches, with an eye always out for the slightest signal, knowing that even when it came, that even when one of *those* agreed, accepted, took him up on it, nothing was going to change, nothing was going to be solved, no peace, no happiness or repose was he going to find, even there, there too, that imposing, imperative figure sprang up, pointing at the sky, and on sidewalks, on street corners crawling with police or official blackmailers, informers, stool pigeons, *agents provocateurs,* even there, there too, she stood, pointing, and in public restrooms, at fairs, at every dangerous proposition accepted with no preliminaries, even at every audacious underwater groping out in the waves at beaches where well-turned, rotund, uninhibited swimmers still went, and every time he let his hand drop in the crowded bus, with a lazy, almost distracted movement, even there, there too, was that tall, serious, respectable figure, and she was pointing, maybe to mock him, maybe to make fun of him, maybe to have her revenge on him, to assert herself, to have her own way, pointing toward the brightest star . . . but it was only much later, long afterward, during one of his hell-bent transits through the stacks of the library, where as often as not he was in pursuit not exactly of a book, that as he was leafing out of simple curiosity through a volume titled *Astronomy for the Fairer Sex,* Arturo discovered, with sad chagrin, that that star, that sputtering match-head at the crest of the hill, the

evening star, his mother called it, or some such name, that that
star was called, so the book said, Arcturus—Arcturus, Arcturo,
Arturo, oh, Arturo, everything is so absurd, he thought furiously, and he put the book back on the shelf, in the wrong spot,
such an uncouth thing to do; but suddenly they ceased, the
magnificent sounds, the enchantment ended, the spell went up
in smoke, an explosion of applause, and Arturo found himself
once more in the great spotlit hall, surrounded by sweaty fags
bobbing to their feet and shouting, *Bravo! Bravo!*, so he availed
himself of the collective enthusiasm to dry his eyes, his tear-riven
face, and after the conductor wended onstage and off again
several times through the maze of music stands, and made the
whole orchestra rise to its feet, they all, the others too, began to
file out of the theater, all so very impressed, as the air now filled
with words like "fabulous," "superb," "divine," but Arturo had
no idea what his opinion should be, much less how to express that
opinion, and in fact he thought it would have been an act of
presumption, or pettiness, to indulge in interpretation, analysis,
synopsis, of what he had heard, enjoyed, lived through, of what
had been revealed to him, even if, which was most unlikely, he
had had a brilliant opinion; as they came to the exit there was a
disturbance of some sort, there were shouts, someone started
running down the street, there was a shot, but only when it was
already too late did Arturo and his friends realize that this was
one of the more and more frequent "roundups" of young men
being carried out these days under the absurd pretext that one
young man's hair was too long, or that another wore clothes of a
certain cut or (most fatal) exhibited certain telling traits, had
certain "mannerisms" . . . and so, one by one, as they passed
through the doors, they were "selected," arrested—Arturo's
friends were pulled in even before he was, and they gestured and
gesticulated, they protested, they tried to get off, get out of it, get
away, using the very voices and postures that had sentenced them
beforehand in the others' eyes, the eyes of the police, but when

they were led away, or dragged, to the machine-gun-guarded bus, Arturo didn't say a word, he never protested, not a sign of annoyance escaped him, even when one of the soldiers made some obscene joke about the hair this straight arrow found immorally long, no, he tranquilly allowed himself to be searched and herded onto the bus, by now full—tranquilly because even as they started the motor, even as the bus pulled away from the theater, even as it was passing the outskirts of the city, heading for one of the work camps, Arturo was still hearing that unearthly melody, and it still had the power to transport him, lift him and float him away, *water,* he had to put more water in, multiply the waters, water in high transparent tubs, under crystal domes, water in tubs, bowls, vats, birdbaths so high that the birds could drink without ever descending to the ground, water in huge elevated pans, in trays, in troughs, lit from within so that one could watch at any given moment of the day or night the graceful swirlings of a fish—or thousands of them—so beautifully shaped and exotically colored that one would gaze amazed, and pools of it, fountains, with statues and falls and goldfish ponds, and aquariums, and sparkling, serpentine, meandering canals, poured into the landscape; *water,* he thought, and throughout the land the capacity of cisterns and reservoirs increased, water flooded moats and streamed into greenhouses, solariums, the royal spas, and then he cast a monumental spread of branches and broad leaves, a treetop like an inverted chalice spilling green, over the muscular trunks of trees; and when all his work, his life's work, was done, when that labor was completed, then, *then,* over it all, cascades of water, walls of water, the rain in colors, rainbows, pilasters rising, a liquid colonnade of columns, water in deep majestic waves over which he and *he* could sail and, at dusk, when everything was golden, gilded, row back home through the western gate as the locks of the great bridge salaamed in synchronized salute . . . before dawn the cry "On your feet!" rang out, to which was usually annexed the word "faggots," and in less than five minutes they had to get up, get dressed, eat breakfast, and be ready to leave for the field, and as soon as they reached the dirt access road the brigade leader would detail the "personnel," as he called them, so as not to be obliged to use the word "men," and in the furrows between the rows of sugarcane the "personnel" had to dedicate all their strength, their entire will, body and soul, to the one objective—cutting the cane: they were watched, they were forbidden to drink water, they were forbidden to talk to their row partners, they could only address the squad leader through an intermediary, a go-between chosen by the others, and then, immediately after lunch, which was eaten right there in the field, the "personnel" had, *he* had, to start chopping again and keep working till nightfall, till it got too dark to see, and if it rained, why, you worked in water, and if you got sick, why, you could just wait till sick call to get sick—"Do we look like doctors?" the liaison between the "personnel" and the leader would yell—but you could talk on the way back, oh, yes, and that was when Arturo's special hell truly began, because at first he had tried not to have anything to do with them, to go on being himself, to isolate himself, stand off, but they (as in *them*) began to want to get back at him, and they started making reprisals: the Wall, the Virgin Queen, Snow White, the Dreary Widow, were the first names Arturo was called in the camp, then the Sphinx, the Ivory Tower, Our Lady of the Cactus; but Arturo stood all that in silence, which simply rankled them the more, and it rankled the higher-ups, the leaders, the others, too, and then they *really* turned on their scorn and contempt for that little faggot who in spite of his "flaw" had the nerve to try to pass himself off as a decent person; Arturo saw that the others, the men in charge, were amused by this spectacle of "poking fun," this mockery, this torture, especially when the butt of it all was him, and so it wasn't long before they (as in *them,* or "the girls," as they invited you to call them), doubtless furious that their verbal attacks had had so little effect, graduated to physical attacks—such as the rock that landed perilously close to Arturo's body, or the smooth, round cake of cow manure that sploshed all over his face, what a scream that was, what shrieks of affected laughter, then what sugary compassion in honeyed words and looks, who in the world would do such a thing, why, not *me*, me *neither*, how perfectly dreadful, or such as the bottle pitched at Arturo's bunk from out of nowhere at the exact moment the lights were turned out, so that Arturo little by little, or maybe all at once, maybe there was one instant of certainty when Arturo realized, maybe when that boot out of nowhere smashed into his face, when Arturo realized, saw, that indifference was a deadly foe to them (and to the others and the rest and everyone else, for that matter), that is, that vulgarity, imbecility, horror, would not suffer indifference; treason, robbery, insult, murder, you could do anything, and many did, but what you could not do, what was absolutely not allowed, was at the moment of committing the crime (both before and after) to underestimate the immense vulgarity, not take it into account, not submit to it, become part of it . . . no, if you wanted to survive you had to adapt or fake adaptation, as perhaps some of the others had done, some who at this very moment were riding roughshod over him, you had to talk like them, laugh like they did, you had to make the same gestures, move like them, and so, seeing this, Arturo did begin to use that affected, dizzying slang of theirs, begin to cackle and howl with laughter like any ordinary queen, to sing, pose, shadow his eyes and dye his hair and paint his lips with whatever came to hand, make big blue rings around his eyes, all that he did, until he had mastered, come to possess, all the cant, every typical movement and feature of the imprisoned gay world, yes, all that Arturo did, and more, until in time he so distinguished himself by the way he swung his hips in *L'Heure de la Dance*, by his steamy renditions of torch songs in *L'Heure de la Chanson*, by the unique way he fluttered his eyelashes, arched his neck, and extended his hands during *Queen for a Day*, by his audacity with the guards in the guardhouse, that at the next year's pageant when the Queen of the Captive Queers was selected amidst a din of shrieks and cries and a sea of burlap skirts, Arturo found himself elevated to the throne by acclamation, and he sat on a kind of catafalque bedecked with the wildest imaginable assortment of rags and trinkets—bunting for the First Lady—surrounded by a shrill, incessant hullabaloo and hymned by off-key praises to his burlap mantle of office and his crown of hibiscus— heaven only knew how they, how the girls, that is, contrived to grow such flowers—and from then on it was incumbent on him to sing, to enliven parties with his most strident cries, to take part in the collective fornications, with the air, always, of a princess born to the blood, royally bored and jaded; and was that, he thought, what he had been before (before experiencing the *real* terror, contempt, solitude)? was that what the rest imagined him to be, now, and for always, what they really saw? was he to be judged by those ridiculous contortions, that cracked contralto voice, those superficial mannerisms, and remembered and forgotten for them? was that to be, did it *have* to be, the vision, the image the rest had of him? . . . mute attitudes and postures, useless conversations, equivocal gestures, bodies now, animals without the gift of speech, hysterical cackles, libidinous shrieks, infinitely affected poses and twirls, choked laughter or confused howls, all of them sinking, drowning, lost, letting themselves be enslaved, letting themselves be used, corrupted, annihilated utterly, and not complaining, unable to complain, was that him too? was that the image of him that everyone would carry away? was there no way out? could he not even suffer his disgrace, his fall from grace, his misfortune, his fate, with dignity and discretion? could he not be himself even in the moment when he let his terror show? was he forever condemned to live in a world where only frustration made sense and had a place, where the only fitting attitude was burlesque and mockery, where there would always be some vulgar, "clever" expression to deliver the *coup de grace* to any coherent thought that might be accidentally expressed, any show of integrity that might unconsciously slip out? . . . you had to dance, you had to join in the fun, jump on the bandwagon, wail, you had to wiggle your hips like a whore, you had to bend over the furrows like a slave, and your lips always had to be ready to spout some trite, conventional formula, and then at night, if there wasn't a meeting or "volunteer" work, you had to jump the barracks fence, a risky business, and go find a recruit— they were housed some distance away, though it was hardly an insurmountable distance for those who really wanted to get there (especially if you considered that the recruits themselves sometimes saved you half the trip)—and Arturo picked or was picked, went out into the underbrush, and found some, momentary, consolation . . . he adapted, he slowly but surely adapted, and toward the end of that summer, when Rosa came to the camp for a visit, Arturo had to make a great effort to control himself, he didn't want to make any gestures that might be misunderstood (understood?) by her, he wanted to speak at his normal pitch, and Rosa looked at him fixedly, inalterably, she had brought him a box of candy, some school notebooks, she gave him some money and at last she hugged him, and what most pleased Arturo about the whole visit, what he bore up under best of all, was the fact that his sister didn't ask him a single question, before it got dark she simply got up and left, she didn't even say she'd come back again to see him, that was some faint hope by now; Arturo went a ways with her, to say goodbye, walked with her to the barracks gate where the barbed wire began, and he noticed that one of the guards flashed her the same gesture, the same obscene gesture that they made to him; "You come to see her?" he heard them ask his sister, and then he watched Rosa's young, tired, worn body walk off down the long expanse of dry, dusty lawn—a meadow, a field; back in the barracks he shared the candy with his friends, "My sister is one of the most expensive whores in Havana," he said, and everyone applauded that show of sincerity with words of extravagant praise and began to flaunt their own sisters' stories, not to be outdone, and Arturo modeled, posed, sang a song, and as his grand finale, acted out a long erotic poem famous throughout the camp, composed right there, in fact, by seven cultured fairies, and then, just before dawn, he collapsed virtually exhausted on his bunk: *he had to destroy himself, like always he had to destroy himself,* and suddenly he jumped up and began groping through the things Rosa had brought him, because that very night he decided that to save himself he had to start writing, *now,* and so he started writing—let them take refuge in their superficialities, their trivialities, let them band together, cling to each other, shriek, shout, cry, let them forget, or never take into account, that for a long, long time now they had been treated as things less than human, the flag didn't fly over them "because you don't deserve it," the officers told them, but even that didn't seem to bother them, no insult seemed to touch them, they found such treatment logical, by now they were so mired in their disgrace, blinkered by it, that the disgrace was just a natural extension of themselves, inevitable, unchangeable, a sort of life sentence, a curse that went on forever and ever, and so they had their screaming, their way of talking, that stupid slang, and most of all, what most galled Arturo, they had that docility in the face of their persecution, that take-whatever-comes-along meekness, they would do anything, suffer any terror, turn the other cheek to any insult, and immediately include it in their traditions, make it indigenous, incorporate it into the folklore, the customs, the daily calamities, yes, they had a gift for transforming terror into familiar ritual: Arturo had seen some of them punished, made to stand for three whole days in the sun, and when it was over they always had some flippant phrase to trivialize the pain, and when some, many in fact, were "transferred" to a different camp, or so the guards said, though nothing was ever heard of them again, they simply vanished, when those men were transferred nobody complained, no one raised a cry in protest, and there was the day a team of playful young officers buried a prisoner up to his neck on the parade ground and left him there for—how many days was it?—and when they finally dug him up he'd lost his voice and had terrible fever, delirium, and nobody protested that time either, so that at last Arturo thought, I'll bet if the others (the guards, he meant) decided to line every one of them up and have them shot by a firing squad, these prisoners would docilely hold out their hands to have them tied, walk docilely through the camp, halt when ordered to halt, and every one of them, with the inherent ingenuousness (gullibility? trust?) of household pets, would burst in silence, all of them, every single one of them, or all of them but him, because he was going to fight, he was going to rebel, he was going to testify to the horror, tell someone, lots of people, tell the world, or tell even just one person, as long as there was one person who still had an uncorrupted, incorruptible capacity to think, he would leave this reality with that one person—and suddenly the notebooks, the common ordinary spiral notebooks with paper lined in blue, the notebooks Rosa had brought him, began to fill with, to be awash in, a sea of tiny tiny words, almost scribbled, fast, *fast,* and almost illegible, even to him, *hurry, hurry, keep on, keep on, fast*—of course taking precautions, because there were searches, you couldn't keep diaries, "pansy-ass bullshit," said the lieutenants as official justification for going inexorably, unstoppably, and legally through everyone's correspondence—so taking at least minimal precautions, he scribbled in the notebooks, and on the inside covers, along the spines, in the margins and blank pages of Marxist-Leninist manuals and economics books stolen from the Political Section, he furtively, quickly filled them with his tiny scrawl, and when nobody was looking, under the sheets or standing in the stall in the toilet, in line for breakfast sometimes, he even filled the margins of grotesque political posters pasted up on the walls, even announcements *For Internal Camp Circulation* suffered that almost microscopic crablike invasion of virtually indecipherable letters and signs, his labor constantly, incessantly interrupted, yet constant—now, now, not now, now, not now—undermining sleep, eliminating mealtimes, invading the bathroom, and seizing his scarce minutes of rest, while Arturo, it goes without saying, was still taking part in all the fashion shows, orgies, assaults on the recruits' camps, "festivals," outrageous carnivals and corona-tions, still wiggling his hips, shaking his ass, going off into the canefield when the soldier gave him the inarguable sign, still singing every night, or almost every night, in that rusty hooker's voice of his, his bluest, most shocking blues . . . scream, shriek, shake his ass and dance, that was the only way his true labor could go unnoticed—gloomy magnificent caverns, legendary caves into which no wind ever blew, grottoes with oozy walls still untouched by the hand of man, sheltering a year-round mist and fog in which the only sound was the tinkle of a dripping spring flowing under stalactites hanging from the subterranean vault, and farther on, much farther on, a distant glow, filtering down from a high cleft, shining on the mysterious waves of an internal sea, a deep, enclosed ocean, yes, yes, the great caverns that he and *he* would explore were necessary as well, so he hollowed them out then and there, below the grand esplanade, the mouths of the caverns discreetly camouflaged by little hillocks of broom, *keep on, keep on,* and Arturo went on scribbling, scrawling over his comrades' letters from home, stolen at midnight, and over the harsh, insulting slogans of the moment: NOT ONE STEP BACK-WARD! WHEREVER, WHENEVER, HOWEVER YOU COMMAND! HARD WITH THE SOFTIES AND SISSIES! . . . one night he found a trea-sure in the Legal Affairs Office, a whole chestful of the minutes of General Staff meetings, which he unhesitatingly appropriated, and which gave him several weeks' worth of working materials— luck, you had to have a little luck, too, he told himself, and in fact luck seemed to be with him: he wasn't so much in demand these days, they hardly ever called him at midnight anymore to give one of his exclusive renditions, they hardly consulted him about which colors went best with such and such a skin color, or the eyeshadow best for eyes shaped so and so, or the kind of costumes that should be worn for an authentic Hawaiian luau night, but of course Arturo could hardly appear enthusiastic about being over-looked, "neglected," and indeed he had to keep insisting, danc-ing, shrieking, butting into conversations even when nobody asked his opinion, had to make himself forever conspicuous, be everywhere, be into everything, exhaust them, exhaust their need of him, for it was only by being constantly conspicuous and seeming to be everywhere at once, being, in fact, an event unto himself, that he could win the extraordinary privilege of finding them indifferent to him, perhaps even the glory of their forget-ting about him completely . . . which was what he did, or tried to do, and by being so very *present* he at last came to be ignored, and by an even greater stroke of fortune, in December a little teenage gay guy, a mulatto, was "placed" in Arturo's camp, and this teenager sang songs in such a hoarse, tired French whore's tremolo, so sad and sentimental, almost tragic, he wore his Afro-curly hair so completely wild and tinted blue, that he was an immediate sensation, his fame spread like wildfire, they called him Celeste, and he became the focus of every gathering and party, so that Arturo, lucky Arturo, was suddenly granted several hours more to dedicate to his blank pages, he could even spend his breaks in camp revising the next portion of his work, ab-stracted, lost in himself, rapt, in another world, and when he was methodically, furiously cutting cane stalks, no longer inter-rupted now, the soldier standing guard would watch him, but now a little puzzled, he couldn't quite figure out what demons possessed Arturo to work so hard, though he wasn't too con-cerned to find out either, because still he gave Arturo the signal once a week and the two of them, nothing had changed about that, waded out into the canefield toward dawn, and so he went on, he went on, he still performed all his duties, he never missed work, he applauded Celeste, and yet Arturo was writing tirelessly, untiringly, constantly, neither faltering from weariness nor ever seeming any closer to the work's end; but as the new year went on there was a change in him, which though perceived by hardly anyone in camp, much less the soldiers, was decisive: one day when he got up Arturo discovered that he had suddenly become handsome, his face, taut and tanned, had lost those sharp, angular, nervous features, his eyes had become larger and brighter, his lips fuller, his hair had acquired a lively, silky, shiny feel, his neck had grown longer, his whole body had taken on the languid muscular grace of a young athlete, and Arturo would seek out the biggest mirrors, belonging to the boldest and generally ugliest queens in camp, he would stand before any piece of shiny metal—a can, a cooking pot, a tank—anything that would reflect back, however faint, however blurred, his new face; whenever they were working in a distant field and had to be trucked over, Arturo would seize the occasion to study himself, admire himself in the rearview mirror, even if the soldiers laughed at him, even if they beat him, or if they were walking, he lost no opportunity to gaze into a mud puddle, a pothole, any pool of water on the way; and he was handsome, handsome, every day more handsome, he told himself as he touched his body, stroked his hair, closed his eyes, and imagined, saw, his slender supple perfect figure, so different from his old skinny clumsy frame—and them, how was it possible that they hadn't noticed? how was it possible that their mouths didn't gape, that they didn't stand astounded before this transformation? and the others, was it possible that they hadn't noticed the change either, such a change as this?—yet on second thought it was true that every time he walked past the guards now some soldier would cup his groin, rearrange his meat, scratch his balls, and make some obscene sign, but that was probably just habit, a tradition more or less, a way of saying *I'm the macho here,* and often they didn't even look at his face as they made the gesture; and on second thought it was true that once in a while one of the fairies would praise the sparkle in his eyes, or on the way back to camp, playing, kidding around, someone would feel his muscles; and it was true, too, that at their weekly tryst, just at the moment of that sighing sob, the soldier had stroked his hair, but that was nothing, nothing in comparison, nothing to match the transformation, those were such poor, cheap, mean ways of recognizing the exuberance of his new beauty, the wonder of it, that harmony of parts whose whole was he, Arturo; how could they be so cruel, how could they have sunk to such blind egoism, clumsiness, gracelessness, brutishness, as not to see it, not to see the change, or if that wasn't it, how could they be so dishonest, so petty, that seeing it, they wouldn't recognize it, praise it, because if there was anything in the wide world that was obvious, patent, undeniable, it was that he, this here-and-now Arturo, was one of the most perfect creatures in the universe, he was utterly sure of that, absolutely certain, so certain that for the first time in his life he began to fear death, and to doubt the power of words: that terse, glowing face, those long, delicate fingers, the fine-boned hands, that supple, pliant body, that soft, full hair, all for the earth, all condemned to putrefaction, to the tireless, bottomless voracity of the worm, and that was that—but was that *all*? . . . oh, every day that passed was one more day pushing, shoving him toward destruction, every hour, every second, a nudge, a push, a shove, a kick in the ass, impelling him horribly and inexorably toward the useless, monstrous end, to grow old, oh my God, to grow old, to become horrible, worse than horrible, sickening, repulsive, a whining, peevish *object,* a drooling *thing,* a palsied fright, to grow old, my God, *grow old,* and what could words do against that terror, against that most frightening and unbearable terror of all . . . what could they do, no matter how passionately ordered, laboriously, exhaustingly, perilously—and finally futilely—ordered, what could they do . . . against that unbearable truth, the unbearable reality, the other reality, *our* reality, he thought, the only weapon is the creation of a new reality, a new present to eliminate this present present, for it cannot be done with anecdotes or stories, or with catalogues or inventories, or minute analyses, anatomies, dissections, however brilliant and acute, of what has passed, is passing, and is to pass, because all those things simply serve to prop up, put in context, justify, apologize for, testify to—give even more reality to—the reality that we suffer every day, because all those things are no more than variations on the theme of terror, and no variation can do more than enlarge (or focus) its original, for History, after all, does not concern itself with groans, or whimpers, or cries of pain, but with numbers, ciphers, statistics, facts, palpable things, monumental events, it rarely gives a writer a second look, but only those who transform, or efface, or destroy—no, headlines are not for the slave, the conquered, and so what you have to do is overlay the image of what you're suffering with the image, the *real* image, of what you most desire, but not the image, either, the true reality, so true you can taste it . . . *growing old, growing old, oh, growing old,* and for a while he couldn't see how to save himself, for a while he thought that even the fact of going on living was tantamount to a betrayal of life, the most abominable act imaginable, in fact, because it implied not living but patiently suffering an abject, unending swindle, a fraud, a great rip-off that could only culminate in the Greater Rip-off to Come; and even his few desires, when they were satisfied—he would think during that time of his life (the page at last written, the soldier unconsciously stroking his head, the rain shower just as he was dropping off to sleep)—even these wishes come true became grotesque, somehow different, not what he'd wanted at all, even when they were exactly what he'd been dreaming of, desiring most—oh, you had to dominate, you had to stay on top of things, be the master of your fate, bribe time somehow, cheat it, you had to hurry if you were going to escape time's twisted sense of humor, hurry, you had to hurry; and here was the oppressive, offensive heat again, *hurry,* here were the insolent blistering summer days again, that fixed, unwavering glare again, and within the humiliating, withering brightness of that glare, the strident clamor of them; and against the piercing stridency what but silence, and against the piercing glare what but that cool, soft, wide expanse veiled in airy curtains, and against the dusty, dried-out, cracked land, the field stripped of trees, the suffocating canefield, what but gardens and fountains, a stone bench in the green shade, wide blue underwater fields with rows of marine fauna of bewitching shapes—this reality, not that one, this truth, not that one; against the time of them, the others, the rest—horrible, horrible, humiliating time—his time, his own time; against that inferno, that hell, against the heavy gears and the linked, concatenated swindles and the insults that went on and on and on, his own place, his own unique and special place, yes, real, irreplaceable, made to be lived in; and so it was then that Arturo began traveling, began to gain experience and to build on a grand scale, began to *live*—a boulevard lined with wisteria drooping under the weight of bursting blooms, and there he was; a big-game hunt in Alaska, and there he was; the gathering of the lotuses in a lake in China, and there he was; a dangerous, violent, poetic landing on the unimaginable surface of a planet being born . . . God, oh God, and in the season of dew, and perfume, and soft green leaves, the flanks of a magnificent horse seen against a morning of utter plenitude . . . to the *chop chop* of his machete, the machete blows little by little cutting an opening in the canefield for the glare, cutting cane stalks, pitching them onto piles under the fixed stare of the soldiers, he kept on, not feeling the cracking of the angry leaves against his sweat-soaked body, not feeling the stings of the ants that crawled up his boots, held on tight, and pierced his flesh, feeling neither the heat nor the weariness, the tiredness, the exhaustion, no longer feeling any calamity at all, he had, without knowing it, without trying to, to the tune of the blows of his machete, surpassed all the goals, the standards set by the highest authorities, the men

who flashed by the concentration camp in their Alfa-Romeos . . .
at Lake Geneva, where the Countess of Merlin perfected her
vocal technique, where Queen Christina luxuriated in exile,
there he was too, shaking his finger peevishly at the delicately
whitecapped waters, or preaching with careless elegance to a
school of dolphins, or lost in a city in Tuscany, or naked and
charmed at the violence of the desert, or under the shaded
Norman loggias of a blazing coastal city in which a Castilian
youth, exquisite, barbaric, gave him a sign gloriously obscene,
there, there he was, young, absolutely free, infinite . . . streets,
streets laid out almost capriciously, gingerbread-decked gazebos
whose cornices, even footscrapers, were reflected again and
again in the impeccable symmetry of their lattices, and there,
where the path descended to form a small, soft, delicious cul-de-
sac, a soughing grove of supple bamboo . . . they would look for
him—everything was organized with strict, macabre organiza-
tion, supervision, vigilance—so they would look for him, because
there were the others, classified into categories, degrees of
power, first lieutenant, second lieutenant, master sergeant, sergeant, corporal, private, recruit, there was an order, there was
always a strict, strictly preconceived and preordained, legalized,
and—like it or not—respected hierarchy, according to which the
highest man on the totem pole could humiliate the next one
down, and that one the next one, and so on down to them, those
who were humiliated by Everyone and could humiliate no one
because the scale of humiliations stopped there; they would seek
him out, yes, that whole assemblage—that order, that hierarchy—was already set in motion, had begun to march, was
obeying directives from higher up, and they were going to get
him: several hours ago the brigade leader had reported to the
officer in charge of the camp that one of the prisoners was
missing, and the officer in charge of the camp had called the zone
officer, who called the foreman, who before would have been
called "the boss" but who now was in uniform, with a pistol at his

waist, and the jeep full of men took off like a shot through the reddish clouds of dust, and all day the zone officer looked even angrier, more furious than usual, maybe because of the heat, or maybe because for months and months now he'd been stuck in that assignment and the "orientation" from "higher up" never seemed to come down so that he could be transferred to a better post; he walked to the barracks, he called for Arturo several times, prisoner number, bunk number, first name, last name, mother's last name, but in the whole echoing barracks there were only two or three queers pushing brooms back and forth, and they jeered back at him, "She's not here," in those unutterably affected voices of theirs, so the zone officer stalked furiously over to the queens, but they were now wielding their brooms with truly astonishing dexterity, sweeping, shaking out rags, fluffing up pillows, picking up the trash, pretending not to have noticed the presence of the soldier, who, all but stammering in confusion, asked them whether they'd seen Arturo, to which the always queenly girls, forever fluffing and shaking, responded that for hours and hours, "centuries," chirped one, they hadn't seen him, so the zone officer stomped into the Political Section office, at which the silly queens threw down their dust rags and brooms and emitted a prolonged shriek, like a soprano with her tit caught in the wringer, but the zone officer was so furious that he didn't pay any attention to the shrieking, he just started giving orders— suits of bright armor, drawbridges, snapping pennants, barbicans, a chapel sanctuary whose stained-glass roses and arched scenes dispersed the sun's rays in all directions through the gloom, reds, greens, scarlets, blues, and there he was too, with his eyes half closed, captivated by the high vaulted spaces of the nave and the solemn cadences of the organ, whose notes soared upward through the rays of purple, as he himself seemed to, too, soared upward through the shafts of gold, Arturo, Arturo— outside: voices, shouting, uproar, shrieking people, they were calling him, urging him to answer, they were bothering him, why were they bothering him, and little by little the great cathedral faded, first the sacred images and then the chords of the organ were shattered by the voice (the shouting) of the soldier on guard, by the indefatigable shrillness of the choir of the haughtiest and most irksome of the queens, who had still not forgiven him for spurning them, cold-shouldering them, *them,* just to go off and build his own little kingdom; it was only then, when there was no alternative, that Arturo came back, still a little fuddled, a little bewildered, and picked up his machete and started subjugating the stalks as he had been taught to do, making them bend to him, here, in this deafening solitude and stillness, in the creaking, crackling, popping, chopping field, and yet, in spite of everything, he still went on perfecting, expanding, improving his construction methods, extending his journeys day after day, until once, in less than one afternoon, he created a floating garden, several columns carved with complex allegories, some swings and gliders, and up in the aspen trees, tiny white platforms, doll-houses, lovely perfect treehouses for rainy afternoons when he had an urge to return to his childhood; and so he kept on, kept on, he was so skilled at his work that he could erect a complete pagoda (with friezes in oils and elaborate trimmings along the undulant roof) in the time it took everyone else to intone on command the strains of the *Internationale* . . . and when he plunged his hands into the sink of filthy dishwater (for once a week his turn at dishwashing came around), he would fish out glorious painted fans, filigreed necklaces, rings, little gold charms and *objets de vertu* and delicately cut gems that someone, a secret admirer no doubt, had dropped there for him to find; he kept on and on like that, tirelessly constructing, planning, building, making, in spite of the group's claims on him, in spite of the "On your feet!" at five o'clock in the morning and the insistent propositions of the guard, and even in spite of the tall, stern, unchanging figure of the mother who at dusk, when he came back from his exhausting day's work in the canefield, was waiting for him, motionless, in the little cleared yard in front of the barracks . . . and only the eyes of Celeste, swollen, open, bulging out of that completely disfigured face, only those eyes ever made him doubt the efficacy of his methods, only they planted him— once more—firmly in this intolerable reality: that afternoon it had rained so hard that they couldn't work for the mud, so the "personnel" were given permission to go swimming in the river, though Arturo naturally preferred to go back to the barracks, where in total solitude, in glorious silence, he confected memorable masterworks, a stunning variety of columned haciendas with pillared, open porches, interior patios roofed by the violet sky above, swirling seashells, sundials, so many marvels, and so very marvelous, that even when, after frantic, futile efforts to rouse Arturo from his reveries, they threw down before him the body of the drowned little queen, it was hard for Arturo to abandon his domain; but there they were, shrieking and screaming, and there was that stiff swollen body, that black protruding tongue, oh, horrible, there was the dead boy, occupying the dimension of the Absolute, the Real, and wiping out, erasing, Arturo's marble-railed terraces and Morris chairs, Persian rugs and sleighs, seashells and pillars, and even that so familiar image of the sorrel mare running swift through voluptuous meadows . . . there was an hour, after dinner and the shrill mess hall conversations, after the shrieking in the showers, when some of them would go off in groups behind the barracks and others would stroll toward the recruit camp, there was that hour when silence, or near silence, so hard to come by, so precious, would help Arturo slip away, escape, as mutable darkness rising from the land and falling from the sky transformed the poor, strict dimensions of a stone, a tin can, a broken piece of broomstick, into a magic trampoline (a jewel, a treasure chest, a pirate's coffers, an enchanted cup) from which he could spring up into fabulous places, into lands uncharted on maps and globes; but that particular night, no matter how hard he tried, Arturo could not transport himself through

the walls of the barracks, because every time he made the effort
to pull out, sneak away, to escape to his own reality, Celeste's
swollen face fell between him and his retreat: at each door and
window of the barracks that face, its horrible swollen tongue, its
eyes bursting from their orbs, cut off all possibility of escape, and
there was the mother, too, tall, cold, stern, standing smack in the
center of the barracks and pointing at the corpse, dominating
Arturo with her fixed recriminating stare, yet looking at him at
the same time the way you might look at a thing you never knew
the importance of until it was lost, and that gaze—abashed,
afflicted, yet fierce—shrank him, left him impotent, imprisoned, *twice* imprisoned, a prisoner now of immediate reality,
of the insufferable bunks, the work, the hunger, the oppression,
and more besides: a prisoner of his own scrupulous memory, and
of death, so that even when he tried to close his eyes and create a
little flowering border along a walk, just a bit of greenery, the
bruised and battered face stayed with him, and that huge purple
tongue made him wipe out the little flowerbed in haste; and then
he tried, he tried to settle for the soft whisper of leaves falling
somewhere else, anywhere else, but his mother was there sputtering and throwing off sparks in the darkness, ordering him to
come closer, closer, closer to her blackened breast, ordering him
to accept only and exclusively, once and for all, *that* reality, the
one that would always spurn him, as he would always spurn it,
too, and so suddenly he realized, and it terrified him, he stepped
back horrified, suddenly he realized that there was no escape,
that there was no way out, that all his attempts, all his efforts,
had been futile, had been for nothing, and that there were
things—aggressive, fixed, unyielding, unbearable, but *real*—
that he could not escape, and that time, too, was inescapable,
and his times, his generation insulted and made to be stupid, and
there were those backbreaking bunks and him breaking his back
on them, and in no time at all the grating, annoying voice yelling
at him to get up, get out of bed, get going, get into step with a

terror that was now, once he knew it for what it was and *knew* it was insuperable, even more terrifying, and then the thought came to him that the brief respites he had been able to enjoy for a moment or two almost anywhere—the shadow of a tree, the sight of a splendid body, the coolness of water trickling down a dry, thirsty throat—were not really respites at all, they were requisites, requirements, necessities that all calamities, all disgraces, all misfortunes had to respect, observe, so that the person who suffered them might perceive the subtle shades within the suffering and thereby suffer them consciously, completely . . . the whole night long Arturo lay in terror with those thoughts, and only toward morning, a little before the exploding "On your *feet!*" could he at last manage to raise a small, fuzzy tower, but at that very instant he heard a chord, a kind of song, a chant—a whistle?—an almost forgotten cadence that once more possessed him, transported him: someone outside was singing, someone outside was bringing forth that melody, someone who was not, it went without saying, one of them, or one of the others, or one of the rest, yet who was out there singing, once more, once more; and Arturo raised his head, and now the person out there singing was not only singing but actually giving long, high whistles, virile and enthralling, as though he were pulling him, calling him, calling him with music, so Arturo leapt from his bunk and ran to a window, and in the middle of the barracks yard he saw a naked, indescribably beautiful youth leading an invisible orchestra that drew those extraordinary echoing sounds out of the night—and Arturo stood paralyzed at the window, contemplating him, while the boy, whistling, now sprang from rock to rock, through the emaciated flowerbeds they had planted, over the shrubs and bushes, always in time to the music; he leapt joyfully, that manly, merry, almost divine piping pouring steadily from his lips, came back to earth near the grindstone they used to sharpen their hoes and machetes and gave it a crazy spin, leapfrogged over the huge kitchen cauldrons and set them ringing unforgettably, then

jumped into the yard's only tree and danced in its highest
branches, and finally, hands on his hips, he looked into Arturo's
eyes and smiled, floated down to earth, turned, and ran away;
Arturo ran after him, but the boy had already gained the barbed
wire fence and was still going, running between the garbage cans
and disappearing over the warehouse roof, and at that very instant the cry "On your feet, faggots!" boomed through the barracks, and Arturo, still dazed by that vision, that spell, had to run
back to his bunk, and the soldier on duty that day was surprised
(without showing the least sign of it) that Arturo was standing
there so straight, so stiff, without having to be called twice—
such discipline! . . . and all that day Arturo worked like a man
inspired; his coworkers watched him laboring feverishly in the
field, and they winked at each other or by way of a quizzical look
seemed to ask what had got into him, or even made fun of him
aloud, but Arturo heard nothing, he just went on working, and
even though the soldier on guard kept a constant eye on him, in
hopes that Arturo would look his way and see the agreed-upon
signal, since tonight, according to his calculations or his in-
stincts, was their night to go to the canefields, Arturo not only
spurned the soldier's invitation, disobeyed his virtual command,
he also stayed away from the mess hall and the showers, he didn't
even change his clothes, he simply sat in the midst of the
hullabaloo of fairies bustling and fluttering around with rags and
stinking mattresses or shaving their legs for the next Big Show,
simply sat impassive, mute, floating along on the crest of that
chaotic hilarity, sat there still and unmoving until midnight, and
then, when he heard the footsteps out in the yard, he leapt
quickly, catlike, through the window: *he* was there, *there,* laughing, standing naked in a bed of tattered windblown flowers;
Arturo tried to approach him, talk to him, touch him, but the
young man dodged, laughing, leaping, so Arturo motioned him to
come with him to his bunk, and only then did the young man
follow, soberly, solemnly, while Arturo, trembling, led the way,

but when they arrived, the young man turned and fled, he disappeared; but even then Arturo lay awake, alert, waiting for his return, until at last they shouted, "On your feet!" and today too he was the first to be standing stiff and straight before his bunk, and so the day went on; that night Arturo watched the young man perform the same ceremony in the yard, but this time, even before Arturo could make the brief conspiratorial sign, the naked youth faded away, vanished near the window, and the following night, though he flew to the window when he heard the footsteps, Arturo barely had time to see the cool, bright figure of the boy disappearing behind the machine shed; Arturo was dumbstruck, downcast, utterly disconcerted as he turned and almost blindly made his way back to his bunk, but then a thrilling surprise (and joy) ran through him when he stumbled into a young, muscled arm waiting for him there—but it was the guard, the soldier pulling him closer, whispering in his ear, "Let's go, baby, it's been me and Mary Five-Fingers for fifteen days now," and since Arturo returned the soldier's inflamed embrace, the two of them took the path to the canefield, where that night Arturo labored with impassioned and painstaking fury to touch the soldier's every erotic spring—and the soldier let him do it, deigning once in a while (perhaps as a caress) to slap his cheek or neck, until at last both were so exhausted that the officer of the guard almost caught them, spent, half asleep, lying in each other's arms beneath one of the sentry posts in the field, but all this time, even when the pleasure reached such intensity that things around him lost their usual solidity, Arturo never once stopped thinking about the radiant figure of the young man who had danced across the yard in his honor, for him, for him alone . . . and the next day, Arturo thought of nothing else, but however hard he tried to call forth the sight of that delicious figure, however much he strained, the most he could do was see (and then only at moments of greatest inspiration, greatest passion) a distant image, an unreal vision held in his memory, but not the

palpable, concrete, live body laughing, moving, making sounds
and footprints, giving off that smell, that odor, or whistling that
special whistle to make Arturo forget his fear and jump out the
window and run off after him; no, Arturo would have to redouble
his efforts, would have to play on, excite, explore, all the recesses
of his imagination if he were going to bring to himself the real—
definite, rounded—image of his lover . . . and at that the terrible
cry rang out, mosquito nets flew open, and the thin shrunken
mistreated bodies, disfigured by work and hunger, began to crawl
out from between the sheets, growling and chattering bizarrely,
"Is there water or isn't there," "Who's got toothpaste," "Who
stole my towel," "Who swiped my soap," "Which one of you fags
dared steal from me, *me*, Friga the All-Powerful!" . . . the "morning refrain," the same old song, the invariable matin bells, and he
too went through the selfsame daily ceremony, climbed up onto
the truck, climbed down again and started to work, but he had to
do something more, he told himself, still chopping, he had to
organize the facts and events coherently, in the first place check
and recheck, test, probe, find out exactly what had gone wrong,
there, right there, in the midst of the noise and shouting and
glare, the whirlwinds of crackling, snapping cane leaves, he had
to *think*—what error had he committed to make *him,* the delicious one, go away—and as he waited, still chopping, for the
water to come around, as he waited, still chopping, for lunchtime
to come around, as he stood there, white and exhausted, sweaty,
filthy, still chopping, waiting for the order to stop ("That's it. Call
it a day, faggots!"), Arturo, who had still not discovered his error,
his mistake, began to create anew, laboriously, in pain and suffering, and he started with the young man's hands—but what were
his hands like? and his face? the smell of his body? what was the
fragrance of his body like? and what about his eyes?—he couldn't
remember the color of his eyes, and he couldn't remember the
shape of his fingers, maybe all together, all five, maybe his hand,
yes, he could see that, he could see *him,* his whole body, radiant,

naked, absolute, leaping and dancing, walking with him to his
bunk moments before dawn, but when it came to the details,
when he tried to reconstruct each individual part of his body,
each gesture, each movement, the image wavered, flickered, and
slipped away, it faded, it became warped and disfigured, and it
was impossible to pin it down, reach it, hold it, as that ideal (real)
boy dissolved (literally) into memory; and so sometimes Arturo
would spend one whole night on the reconstruction—unsuccess-
ful—of a smile, and then the next day he'd go on with the *chop
chop chop* again, the endless round, cut the cane in three pieces
and toss it on the heap, *chop chop* . . . one night, toward dawn,
moments before the accustomed cry, moments before the moment when with a sick gesture of final exhaustion, a gesture of
final violence, he would have run to the guard, seized his pistol,
and blown out his brains, just moments before that final moment, Arturo had the sudden intuition, felt, and clutched
fiercely at the idea, that if the delicious young man were going to
appear again then he, Arturo, the lover, had to go on building,
yes, go on constructing a place, an ideal place, worthy to receive
him, a fabulous, peerless, wondrous, unparalleled place for the
moment of their meeting, a place so captivating, so seductive,
that when *he* arrived he would never want to leave, he would stay
by his side forever and ever—because after all, didn't he already
know the young man's tastes? hadn't the young man appeared at
the precise instant Arturo recommenced his great project? so
how else was one to interpret that magnificent apparition? wasn't
the young man the culmination of all his efforts, all his creation,
all his skill and art, the ideal inhabitant for the ideal realm?—
and now Arturo understood, he finally saw that the youth was
the capstone to his masterwork, his magisterial creation, the
marvelous final touch that could only be conceived, seen, possessed, when all the other marvels that would house him, shelter
him, delight his senses, had been created . . . and so Arturo
scattered cenotaphs, gargoyles, a great bridge, a flock of gulls

flying seaward in formation, the violence of a springtime bursting
forth amid bright shops full of mirrors and glass, lighthouses,
sunlight-glittering windshields, fields of tall, weedy grasses, and
columns, staircases, gables and pediments, porches, temples,
and the many, changing quarters of a cobbled sky, all this he built
with inexpressible effort, and still *he* did not come, so all those
edifices and monuments, those landscapes, disappeared, Arturo
wiped them out, though still he refused to give up, for if all the
wonders he had created so far had not sufficed to attract *him,*
then it must be that all the wonders he had created so far were
small, mean, cramped, common, and contemptible, not to men-
tion incoherent, because after all, wasn't it true that at precisely
those rare, fugitive instants when something (who knew what)
whispered to him that he had almost, almost achieved perfection
(uncommonness, at least), or something approaching it, wasn't it
then that he felt *him* near?—and at that very instant, Arturo
deduced, he felt the light of realization flooding him, he suddenly
knew that the divine figure not only required his stage, his
pedestal, to offer secluded, beckoning recreations (re-creations),
but furthermore deserved—demanded—a perfect universe, a
unique, unexcelled site, something matchless, superior, worthy
of a prince—a castle! a castle! of course, that was it! that was
what *he* was waiting for (for hadn't *he,* the prince, appeared just
when Arturo had managed to raise a tower?), a legendary, uncharted place, filled with fantasy and fable, dotted with for-
tresses, keeps, martellos, campaniles, magical nooks and
corners—only then would *he,* the unique, the exclusive one,
return and let himself be admired, return, if only to visit; so to
that unheard-of task of construction Arturo gave himself over,
into that work he put his whole life—not moving a finger gratu-
itously, not wasting a single word, not squandering his fury, even
his most indispensable heats of fury, not meeting the daily terror
with passion, but saving his passion, all his forces, all his
strength, for his great work—but things conspired, everything

conspired, everyone kept interrupting him, throwing obstacles in his way, it was all so slow, it crept along, crept along, there was always some new field that had to be cut right this minute, there was always some stand of weeds that had to be pulled, some sidewalk or patio to sweep, some stone to pick up, something to shake out or dust or fluff up, something to put away or pull down, some order to follow, always somebody calling, a call to work, to arms, they are looking for you, they're shrieking for you, they're screaming at you, and the columns dissolve, the magnificent carving of a staircase blurs and fades away, the balusters topple, and the little spiral of water, the sparkling spiral in which tiny glistening silver fishes leap, spirals back again to the depths . . . so you had to deny yourself, you had to escape somehow, it was thwart or be thwarted, stand up or be stepped on, there had to be some solution, some method, something to grab on to and use to carry out his plan, *his plan,* and he knew, he saw, he intuited, that under these conditions he would never achieve his ends, but he also saw, and with even greater clarity, that precisely for that reason he *had* to carry out his plan, because his goal, that plan, was the only thing that justified his life, gave his life meaning, and he saw that time, time, above all *time* was what he needed now, not just the few moments he lay awake in the morning while the others slept, while the others groaned in the prison of their common nightmares or moaned deliriously under their own caresses, and not just the seconds snatched as he stood in line for the bowl of soup, when abstractedly, as though staring at someone, something, nothing, he availed himself of the lull (because sometimes, to his delight, the line moved slowly, slowly, and he could even get all the way *there,* there where his great works were being erected, and he could touch up the expression on a statue's face, tune the resonance of a Renaissance clock bell, or polish the authenticity of a nest of parson birds swaying in the high thatched greenness of the pine grove), no, those brief moments were no longer sufficient, they just weren't enough, it was time to go back again, he had to go back, the truck was already waiting, and again and again the "Hurry it up, you jerk, or you'll lose your turn," or the "On your feet, assholes, time to get back to the field," or the "What's wrong with you today, don't feel like modeling with the rest of the girls?" or even the soldier's lascivious gesture (those gestures), and suddenly the nest stopped swaying, the lake was not yet fringed with trees leaning out over it to look at themselves in its limpid waters, and the racket of plates and spoons blotted out, drowned out, drowned once and for all the whisper of wind-blown stalks of grain and even the fragrance of a row of cape jasmines so doggedly devised only a few hours earlier, and he had to pull back his bowl ("Next! Next! Come on, girls!" the cook was screaming) to keep fragments of his shattered construction from dropping into it, and so the ladle discharged its load into the void, and now the cook was screaming, *You faggot, you did that on purpose, now you can eat shit!* and suddenly the whole line started moving, protesting, stamping and shouting, the extremists screaming, *Lynch 'er, lynch 'er, lynch 'er,* until even the roses, so beautifully, perfectly crafted and set down there beside the picket fence, had lost their delicate shape in the spreading pool of steaming soup . . . time, time and silence, that was what he needed if he were going to triumph, that was what was essential if he were going to win the battle, give meaning to his life, keep on; time—steal some time for himself, appropriate a little time and silence so he could finally achieve his goal, his one and only goal, the goal that allowed him at least for the moment to stand all these horrors, because he *had* to win that battle, constantly lost, against time, he *had* to impose the refinement and fecundity of silence on the sterile stupidity of this never-ending, perpetual racket—oh God, God, give me time, grant me the time I need, lend me, please, time enough—but God had disappeared some time ago, committed suicide, taken a powder, *poof!*, and was gone in a cloud of smoke, like so many sweetnesses, terrors, and dreams, so now there was nobody but

him, Arturo, to be God, and nobody but him, Arturo, who could
do anything for him, Arturo; now and forever, once and for all,
whatever hell he was stuck in, him and his terrible unhappiness,
him and the insults, him and his uncommon, unsuspected,
unimaginable dreams, he had to flee it, run where no one would
bother him, where no one would rape his landscapes and ravage
his monuments, flee to a place where he would never again have
to perform the enslaving meannesses that every man, everywhere, was suffering now, now and forever, simply so he'd be able
to fill—or half fill—his belly, or fall into bed and sleep, or
fornicate and engender, multiply the numbers of these grotesque,
imperfect, screaming, dirty, evil, vile, cowardly beings: them,
the others, the rest, all of them . . . he couldn't go on just taking
it, he would not allow his glorious images, the magnificent con-
structions, the beautiful, grand, divine projects swelling inside
his head and desperately crying to come out, pour forth, and
grow, would not allow them to be disfigured or lost, just at the
moment when he should be putting them into execution—no!
because even if before, up to now, he had resigned himself to
short escapes, hiding close to camp and scurrying back when his
absence was noticed, he could never be content with that again,
because now it was his life, it was his time that mattered to him,
and he wanted it *all,* not just a few measly, niggardly minutes: his
time, his real time, his great and glorious time, without one
single shriek, scream, or piercing wail, without a single order or
insult, without anyone in the world but Arturo himself and the
fabulous project in gestation, so that at last *he* would come, would
visit him, would stay—the other; and at that moment of full and
final realization Arturo threw down his machete and ran through
the canefield, panting but free, until he reached the esplanade,
that vast space where he would give shape to his domain—the
immense, wonderful castle—far removed from any terror; and
instantly, at his behest, the wondrous, peaceable, palpable figures of the elephants began to descend, and he set them down

slowly, carefully, at the end of the broad plain, and then feverishly set about constructing everything requisite for the grand
reception, for the arrival of the other, of *him,* who would be, at
last, the crown and culmination of his work . . . but then, now, at
this very moment, in the Political Section office, the officer of the
guard has received the information from the zone officer, who in
turn received it from the soldier on duty, and the officer of the
guard stands, rests his hand instinctively on the butt of his pistol,
and says, "So the little pansy is playing AWOL again, huh?" and he
gives the first lieutenant the order for pursuit and capture, and
the first lieutenant passes it along to the second lieutenant, the
second lieutenant repeats it to the master sergeant, the master
sergeant barks it to the corporal, and the corporal, with a crew of
picked soldiers, embarks on the hunt—but first the first lieutenant orders a search of Arturo's ratty belongings, at which everyone, eyes alight in expectation of cigarettes, money, maybe a can
of condensed milk, maybe even jewelry ("You never know about
these fags"), begins rummaging: "Letters and photos of more
faggots," says one, and strews them on the floor; "Face cream,"
says another, and smashes it against the wall; and papers, papers,
pieces of cardboard, placards, posters, signs, announcements
and orders from High Command, papers, papers, and more
papers, and all of them written all over, scribbled, marked,
scrawled on, out to the very edges: "Those minutes we'd thought
were lost," the lieutenant says, "what's that goose doing with the
minutes!" and he picks up a piece of paper and reads, not without
difficulty, then instantly, disgusted, he looks at the corporal and
hands him one of the hen-scratched documents—"What'd I tell
you," he says, "with these people you've gotta be on your toes
every minute, because this guy wasn't satisfied just demoralizing
himself, he wanted to demoralize all of us, the whole country, *his*
country, *your* country, look at this, look what he's written here—
counterrevolution, open, bald-faced, brass-balled, faggot
counterrevolution!"—and so the corporal reads, not without dif-

ficulty, and stumbles on words he has never seen or heard before: *jacinths, turquoise, onyx, opals, chalcedony, agate, jade . . . a half-frozen pter-o-dac-tyl*—"Pterodactyl! What the fuck is that! Have you ever heard such nonsense, such gobbledygook, can you believe this gibberish! I never saw such words . . . so it's true," he says, "we've hit the jackpot, men," but he thinks: so this is all it takes, this scribbling, this diarrhea of the mouth, this is all it takes to get your head chopped off—and he even stands there a moment lost in his thoughts, his eyes on the page though he does not see, read, or understand the deluge of words, the words scrawled in a tiny, fiendishly difficult hand; because really, as far as he's concerned, there's basically just one enemy, a man with a gun who wants to fight, and everybody else, he thinks, the rest of 'em, he thinks, are just faggots like this guy, they're not going to overthrow any government; but then his eyes focus, he raises his head, he hands the papers back and salutes according to regulations and barks, "I'll bring him back, sir," and charges out with his men . . . where just a moment ago there had been cramped spaces, hallways so narrow that you had to back into a doorway to let someone pass, now there were immense spaces, enormous, wide and bright, there were high, curving, splendid vaults; where just a moment ago there had been the smallest possible rooms, closed, hot, fetid hovels, crowded and dark, now there were limitless rooms, bedrooms and studies and music rooms and salons without end, airy apartments with harmoniously proportioned glass doors opening onto wide terraces bathed by a soft southern sun, and greenhouses, solariums, aviaries—crystal rooms of filtered light; where just a moment ago there had been blotched and smeary walls crumbling and flaking from the explosion of a worn-out sugar boiler or groaning under the weight of the plastered-up placards his eyes had always spurned yet were always condemned to see, now there were thick, solid, imposing walls, towers rising proud into the sky, scraping the undersides of the clouds; where before there had been a burning, glaring stand of cane, the dusty squeezed-dry landscape, scrawny, windblown weeds poking up out of a pile of cans and streamers of used toilet paper, now there were tall, strong trees, majestic trees with shade, trunks ten good men could not put their linked arms around, trees whose feathery green whispering leaves could shelter an army—*his* army; where not a moment ago he had been standing in line for a drop of water, "Hurry up in that shower before the tank runs out," drawing a bucket from a well a mile away, bathing in the filthy puddle you had to drink out of too (like some animal), diving in and out again, quick, before they came with their "*I* want to cool off" and muddied the place up worse, now there were deep expanses of blue, vast and mysterious expanses, motionless undulating expanses solemnly crisscrossed by high supple bridges, ships with sails of scarlet or royal purple, bellied out like a giant's roseblooms, and great rocky breakwaters radiating out from the castle—for it was a castle, rising above it all, that he had to erect, at the exact center of the grand esplanade, a solid, magisterial bulk, with towers and posterns and cloisters, crowning and commanding the whole, that was what he had to construct so that the exquisite youth would appear—as foretold by all the signs he'd so far seen—so now he opened out the gates of the palisade beside his monumental barbicans, he multiplied the flanking towers, raised the height of the vallations, the breastworks, the lunettes, extended salons and halls and widened watchtowers, scattered corbels and trusses, threw up buttresses and parapets, cut tiny loopholes, erected obelisks in homage to the great; standing high on a merlon on the crenellated battlement, he inserted two embrasures in the wall, and peeking out a bull's-eye, he doubled the fortifications leading out to the ramparts, and then he stood erect on the pinnacle of a parapet and changed the color of the deep waters of the moat, tinkered with the convoluted goldsmithing of the footscrapers, blackened the carriages of the cannons . . . and still he went on working, placing rooms here and there, setting imperial cornices in place, building stairways with treads and risers in hundreds of different styles, adding cupolas, pergolas, steeples, lecterns and music stands, leather armchairs, eaves along which banners snapped and waved, commodes with brass fittings, dormers and gables and captain's walks and arcades, embellished with spandrels and cutwork fans, scrolls and spindles and knobby turned grilles, brackets and mouldings and balustered handrails; and then he leapt up onto the highest, grandest cupola and set the weathervane that would tell which way the wind blew; and now he built great floating decks, pavilions, salons with windows on the water, rooms so grand that to open a door one had to solicit the aid of at least two armies; and he created, too, fabulous realms, unimaginable realms rife with magical flowers that transformed themselves into instruments of pleasure, and he created artificial heavens, a velvety little theater of such perfect acoustics that the death throes of a fly (had it occurred to him to create such an insect) would have set off a chain of concatenated echoes, and in the theater he placed a harpsichordist of such virtuosity that when his supple fingers touched the keys they brought forth immortal melodies, melodies so transporting that they raised the theater's curtains as he, Arturo, made his entrance into all the halls, the salons, the grand rooms, ah, the music, once again, once again, the long-held chords, the rising and falling of the music, again and yet again, its cadence, its rhythm, the music's measured step, the enchantment, the spell, the flood of music over him; it was the same music he had heard the night of the roundup at the theater, the same music he had heard in the barracks moments before *he*, the divine youth, appeared to him, and the music commanded, ordered, impelled him to go on with his magnificent construction, and accompanied him in it, led him to seek complete perfection, a culmination absolute and impossible ever to achieve again . . . libraries, grottoes, bandshells and amphitheaters, bronze scales, secret passageways, batons and the wellheads of wishing wells, palanquins, veloci-

pedes, barouches, cabriolets, cameos, and a round little, fat little
brigantine whose silhouette against the lighter sky bobbed softly
on a mirrored sea, and down to the ship-laden harbor from the
citadel led a yellow canal cut at intervals by chased and carven
locks—and there were pitchers and urns, flowers, perfumes,
unfurled bolts of fabric, burning-glasses, jacinths, turquoise,
onyx, opals, chalcedony, jade, agate, hematite, jewels, gems unimaginable, bijoux, every precious bauble in the world, chrys-
olite and chrysoprase, girasol, the most lustrous and luxurious,
the most costly, the strangest and most rare, the most peerless
and irrepeatable, jewels, jewels, and even a diamond cutter set in
a moonstone coffer, for the sole purpose of polishing nuptial gems
. . . but he caught himself up, for there were still so many
marvels to be made—sandy beaches, orchids, hollows and glens
and Patrocluses—for his was a delirium of creation, he was
spellbound, entranced with the pleasure of making, his was the
power to do all, the power to be part of all, the power to suddenly
step back from, cast off, rise above tradition, the mean and
common past, the mean and common curse, the usual and unending woe of the world, the power to break, once and for all,
with that shadowed and shadowy, stooped, poor, scared, tired,
enslaved figure which he had been (and which still was them, the
others, the rest, all of them) and to be free, God, to create the
dreamt-of, yearned-for universe, *his* universe . . . sometimes he
would suddenly erect an imposing church, for the sheer pleasure
of adding numberless triforia to it—galleries, mezzanines, tran-
septs, open clerestories; sometimes his zeal was such that he
forgot to bother with even the merest hint of coherence and he
would plant a cherry tree next to a mantelpiece clock, set a Bali
dancer in the crown of a coconut palm, place a Manchurian stork
on top of a Gothic credenza, above the high weathercock put a
pterodactyl so disoriented in its new world that it flew about in all
directions, and even craft a tapir whose cold-forged, riveted
reflection shone in the enameled walls of a huge Byzantine hall

with Moorish-Islamic mosaics—porticoes, bull's-eyes, gilt black-amoor statuettes and flambeaux, needlepoint tapestries, tartans, and post chaises, all were created and multiplied, all the richest, all the most exotic materials, all the most fetching, seductive, attractive, beguiling objects, all the loveliest things of the earth were necessary, surely, if *he,* the exquisite youth, were to make his appearance; and in the parks, down the long allées, in the great stately gardens, under statues carved with painstaking art: peaceful figures strolling along beside the monuments and *memento mori* to the end of time, lockets left lying on a sundial, breviaries in a hermit's cave no one will ever enter, tiny birds minutely wrought, woven into pink trumpet trees in constant flower, leaves, the rough forest floor carpeted with leaves and thatched with the aerial roots of cupped bromeliads, the little domed tower of an observatory rising from a hummock of softly curved palms, white paling fences and pebbles beside the rain gauge, and a little farther on, among the verdure of the shivering cool bamboo, deep in the green, the wetness bursting with seeds, great bird's nests dangling purselike from the trees, the splendor of blackness yielding itself up to fireflies and the gleaming shine of rats: the woods, the woods, the horn, *ta-raa,* the hunting horn, those grand, imperial, peaceful, idyllic sounds, sonorous echoes through the halls of the forests, and those perfectly ordinary, voluptuous, peaceful mornings, the woods, the woods, flaunting the vision-inducing range of color of the ocean itself, and like the ocean swaying, crooning, whispering a kind of lullaby, and rocking him, the woods, the woods, tiny things, enormous beetles and moths, imperturbable hovering little creatures, and the reflection of the universe in a raindrop cradled in the fold of a velvety elephant-ear leaf, a universe governed not by trite, clichéd, mean and changeable laws, but rather by the inalterable, divine laws sanctioned by instinct, intuition, and the rhythm of life—the precision of rainfall, the harmony and balance of the spheres—all of which had nothing whatever to do with the

hysterical, capricious, blind and dirty path laid down by cackling
fate for that shadowed and shadowy, stooped, poor, scared, tired,
enslaved figure which he had been (and which still was them, the
others, the rest, all of them) . . . the earth, waiting, penetrable,
moist, offering witness to the age-old tickle-and-coo, emitting an
exhalation, a sigh, a murmur, a breath, the earth, the earth, and
there, in a clearing, very near the water, among vines and lianas,
a jasmine plant, a piece of cloth, a veil, a virgin in the timeless
ecstasy of a dance consecrated to the flower—it was he, he, it was
Arturo dancing, it was he who danced, danced, there in the
center of the wood while he awaited *him,* danced in the slanting
ray of sunlight that filtered through the treetops and made a soft
shimmer on the ground . . . but was that the sound of running
feet?—it was the dense drapery of the branches stirring and
fanning a breeze so that he would know that they too awaited *his*
arrival—and who made that echoing cry, that murmuring cry?—
it was the numberless leaves on numberless branches, the sprites
and demons of the air, the gods of the wind who, also waving,
waited—and now, that constant, rising drumming, from where
did it arise?—it was the tiny creatures, crickets, caterpillars,
worms, ants, and beetles, the tiny beasts of the skin of the earth
who begged not to be excluded from the reception, who had come
to see *him* pass—but what was that incredible noise over beyond
the rocks?—it was the water, the green, perfumed, and ceremo-
nious, solemn, glorious water standing aside, parting so that *he*
might pass, so that he and *he* might at last stand face to face,
parting to be the patron of his self's best definition . . . and
Arturo heard that swelling sound, that murmur, those rhythmic
steps, the soft, tentative steps of all beings, even of all things,
which somehow—how?—spoke to him and announced with joy
that *he,* the godlike youth, was coming, drawing near, yet even
in his inexpressible happiness, in the midst of his joy unbounded,
Arturo felt a kind of sadness for those other trees, the ones that
he had not created, the ones that stood waiting for the axe, and

his heart was shaken by the flotsam and detritus of seaborne bottles, discarded newspapers, bits of chaff scudding in the wind . . . but wasn't it time now to enter the castle? wasn't everything marvelously and finally complete now? were there not rivers, woods and forests, lakes, seas, ever unfolding skies and sumptuous pavilions set in gardens? was not everything perfectly disposed and balanced?—and all that was lacking now the nuptial suite, the marriage bed, the curtained alcove?—and so now, in one graceful leap, he came to the path before the castle, he walked up the causeway to the gate and went inside, and he made his way to the residential quarters, where he chose a large apartment in an angled corner with a view across the entire realm and a door that opened out onto a hanging terrace, and in the apartment Arturo set a curtained bed, a carpet, a table with a vase of roses, two candelabra, and a mullioned window softly veiled and shuttered by a lattice, with an awning of fine canvas to protect them from the sun on days of glaring heat, and Arturo wished for climbing flowers to twine up through the lattice and into the room, and there were flowers, and then two easy chairs, yes, the room needed two soft chairs, and then, at last, he walked through the apartment, through all his creation, and saw that it was good, this ample and commodious space, furnished with spare elegance, airy and calm, everything well calculated to surprise, delight, and, seducing, soothe—could anything be missing still? . . . Arturo suddenly began to feel a floating sensation, as though his feet did not have to touch the ground for him to glide along, and he stood there like that for a while, perfectly alert yet awestruck, amazed, floating, flowing, swaying, turning in the luminescent brightness that did not shock but soothed his eyes, and then he came back down again and sprawled across the bed; lying there, he studied the diverse combinations of colors that bloomed and faded away again beneath the mullioned windows, like a constantly shifting kaleidoscope of light, and then he closed his eyes and thought: this room was the most wonderful thing in all his work, and yet he felt a strangeness in it, he had just the slightest feeling that something was lacking for the chosen one at last to come, and so he thought, and he thought, and he thought, he kept on meditating as his gaze rested on the great vista that unfolded beyond the castle . . . perhaps what it really needed was not more furnishings but a ship, a ship made of crystal and gleam, in which, if one wished—if he and *he* wished—they could leave even this place one day . . . and so another place, too, another enchanted place was needed, a get-away, a place filled with glimmering rays of light, violet, golden, red, a place of tightropes and funiculars and other inventions hitherto unknown even to themselves: moors, and above them, mad-eyed, barbaric, livid moons far up in the sky gilding animals below of archaic, burnished, heraldic mien, sky after sky after sky, and so many secret passageways to slip down, if one wished, away to the ends of the earth . . . but over there, shouldn't there be some other kind of tree?—a tree that could tiptoe, quick, from here to there, because Arturo often felt so sorry for things stuck in one place all the time, out in the rain, the cold, the heat and sun, the danger . . . and oughtn't there be a sea of spume, too, nothing but froth, all sea spray, so that someone, so that he and *he,* could dive in and touch and be touched by pure, sheer effervescence? . . . and at the mere thought, the trees broke out in a sound like uprooted earth, and that sea was formed, and yet still *he* did not come, to take Arturo by the hand and lead him down to plunge into that ocean of spray . . . but maybe what was really needed was not a sea of spume but a long clothesline hung with sheets snapping in the breeze, lovely, lovely sheets, white, fragile, starched, between which he and *he* might roll and twist, clean sheets like his mother's white cotton slips, which he used to pull over his head, like this, and feel the warmth of her loins . . . lovely, lovely sheets, white, fragile, trembling, new-washed and smelling of soap, new-dry, floating in the sun, the lift and pop and fluttering down of the breeze-blown sheets, like this . . . oh, and angels, angels, oughtn't there be angels too? might it not be precisely angels that would summon his beloved?—a choir of angels, a shining choir of angels to announce *him*, squads of angels, blond, winged, fresh-scrubbed cherubs who, thankful for having at last been given real existence, would bear witness to *his* arrival . . . but that sound? that music, that riot of brass, those echoes, harps and tambors, viols and flutes and clarinets, that rolling of drums, the hymn?—wasn't that them, the angels, now at last proclaiming (the trumpets! the clarions!) that the chosen one, the longed-for, the divine youth, was making his entrance, that *he* was there, here, accompanied by the choir of angels—the hallelujah—and only waiting for Arturo to come out of the castle to verify with his own love's eyes that *he* did, in fact, in fact and in reality, exist?—yes, it was *he,* the hitherto ungraspable, the being of his dreams only, the being who had appeared to him, naked, smiling, beckoning, and ordered him to build that marvel, that grand imposing castle, it was *he,* the god, his god, who now, radiant, smiling, came; so there was no reason to wait a moment more, the edifice was built, the flags were snapping from the parapets and eaves, and the choir of angels (that last prerequisite) was floating down from heaven to attend the presentation . . . and now the hymns were sounding, the cornets, the song of earth and heaven, you could hear it, now almost at hand, and to the riot of metal—cymbals, drums—they came, they came, bearing the shining treasure . . . and Arturo quickly ran through the suite, across the cantilevered terraces, the royal courtyard, and up to the corner towers, and bracing himself against a postern, vaulted the palisade gate, landed on a battlement, and flew out over the moats, disdaining the drawbridge . . . and there they were!— there was the troop of angels, marching toward him, angry and dripping with sweat, for they had been running for more than four hours, trying to catch that faggot deserter, but there he was, about time, and look at that moron come running toward us— now, thought the sergeant, choking with fury and suffocating in the heat, now that you know you're trapped (*lost*) out here on this nice flat land, you think you'll come to meet us, and so here you come, huh, you shit bastard, and he raised his weapon and aimed, regretting for an instant that Arturo wasn't running the other way so he could justifiably fire on him, and unable at last to contain himself, he screamed, "You faggot, just let me catch you, your ass'll be raw meat, you can either make yourself into a man here, or you're screwed!" . . . and at that, the music, the magnificent music, the choral chant of the angels, suddenly ceased, and Arturo discovered himself running toward a squad of soldiers advancing slowly toward him with rifles at their chins, and for a moment he was paralyzed, the notes of the hymn hung in the air, in his memory, but only for a moment, because as soon as he looked carefully at the group of armed men he saw with irrefutable, inarguable clarity that the man at the procession's head was not one of the camp's many first or second lieutenants, all of them the same—all servility with their superiors, all arrogance with the prisoners—but his mother, Old Rosa, boiling mad, in uniform, gun in hand, screaming at him, *Faggot faggot faggot, you won't get away from me this time*—howling, Arturo staggered back a step, then staggered back again, and then he turned and ran, ran madly, knocking over pilasters and pillars, toppling statues, trampling beds of flowers, and only when he was past the castle moats, running on beyond the watchtower on the far wall, did he turn and look back, but still he saw Old Rosa, gun in hand, dressed like a soldier, and he saw too, there among the anonymous, obedient, all-the-same soldiers with their impenetrable faces, the face of the divine youth, the one for whom this castle had been built, the young man radiant in his faded uniform, but he too was raising his rifle, aiming it at him . . . *Faggot!* boomed a soldier's masculine voice, perhaps the divine youth's, *we've ordered you to halt three times—this is your last chance! Halt or we fire!*—but Arturo, turning quickly away, flew toward the horizon, leaving flagstaffs, gazebos, parasols, herbariums, cameos in ruin, obliterating pools of water, and even knocking over the solitary rain gauge and startling the pterodactyl, which had been perched there watching the troops advance . . . and it was not until Arturo reached the monumental row of stately, regal elephants that the bullets struck him down at last.

Havana, 1971

Author's Note

The dedication "For Nelson, in the air" refers to my friend Nelson Rodríguez Leyva, the author of a lovely children's book of short stories, *El Regalo* ("The Gift"), published in 1964.

In 1965, Nelson was imprisoned in one of Cuba's homosexual prison camps—this one in the province of Camagüey—known officially by the name Military Units for Aid to Production (UMAP). After three years of forced labor, Nelson was released on grounds of "mental illness." In 1971, in desperation, he used a hand grenade in an attempt to hijack a Cuban National Airlines plane to Florida. Overpowered, in fear of being assassinated by the military guards on the plane, he threw the grenade, and it exploded. The aircraft, however, managed to land at José Martí International Airport in Havana. Nelson and his friend and traveling companion, the poet Angel López Rabi, age sixteen, were shot by firing squad.

Nelson left an unpublished book of stories about his experience in the concentration camp. That book apparently "disappeared" at the hands of the Cuban authorities. A few university libraries in the United States have copies of *El Regalo*.

A third person, the writer Jesús Castro Villalonga, who was not on the plane but who knew of the plan, was sentenced to thirty years in prison. He is still serving out this term in La Cabaña, in Havana.

I often think of that moment when, grenade in hand, flying over the Island with its concentration camps and jails, Nelson, in the air, at last felt free, perhaps for the only time in his entire short life. Hence the dedication of this book.

As for the original manuscript pages, which I wrote in Havana in 1971, they may be seen in the manuscript collection of the library at Princeton University, Princeton, New Jersey.

New York, 1984